My folks didn't approve of my going door to door. They had both offered me work at their offices for the summer, but I couldn't see being with either of them for eight hours of work and then at home. What they had really wanted to do was put me on display for their coworkers. *Speak, son. Be Afro-American Intelligence at its best, son. Blow honky's mind, son.* The last thing they wanted to do was let it be known that I was selling cookies and candy. It wasn't dignified. It wasn't brag worthy. But I liked it. I was good at selling. Getting the door open. Reading the customers' faces. Knowing which pitch would work. Selling to diabetics and koshers. Stealing High Man bonus away from this dude Carmello, who had everyone awestruck. I wanted to dethrone him.

Other Bantam Starfire Books you will enjoy

RITA WILLIAMS-GARCIA

FAST
TALK ON A
SLOW TRACK

Blairsville High School Library

BANTAM BOOKS
NEW YORK · TORONTO · LONDON · SYDNEY · AUCKLAND

*No character in this book is intended to represent any actual person;
all the incidents of the story are entirely fictional in nature.*

RL 6, age 12 and up

FAST TALK ON A SLOW TRACK

*A Bantam Book / published by arrangement with Lodestar Books,
an affiliate of Dutton Children's Books,
a division of Penguin Books USA Inc.*

PUBLISHING HISTORY

*Lodestar Books edition published 1991
Bantam edition / December 1992*

ISBN 0-553-29594-2

Published simultaneously in the United States and Canada

*Bantam Books are published by Bantam Books, a division of Bantam
Doubleday Dell Publishing Group, Inc. Its trademark, consisting of the
words "Bantam Books" and the portrayal of a rooster, is Registered in
U.S. Patent and Trademark Office and in other countries. Marca
Registrada. Bantam Books, 666 Fifth Avenue, New York, New York
10103.*

PRINTED IN THE UNITED STATES OF AMERICA

OPM   0   9   8   7   6   5   4   3   2   1

for the '75 NOAH freshmen, especially eternals

RETURN OF THE SON

"*Denzel, come to the front of the class. Take off your face. Show the class your face. Denzel, we're waiting. Take off your face.*"

I WAS thrown clear from the cloudy dream border and landed on a small bed. The bed sheets, once neatly tucked beneath the mattress, had been ripped out. I still clenched snatches of white cloth in both fists, as though holding on would anchor me safely to this world. It didn't work. I had gone and come back and my heart wouldn't stop pounding. I was losing control and I couldn't stop shaking. IT stared me in the eye and was going for my face.

I searched through the muted shades of the room, making sure IT was gone. Real. The room was real, and I was really in my bed. The desks, bookshelf, and dressers were in the same spot they had stood for the past six weeks. Arnold, my roommate, was asleep in his bed, snoring louder than usual.

I let go of the sheets and lay my head down, wiping the perspiration from my face into the pillow. I remained stiff, watching the room, Arnold, our suitcases, and the door for as long as I could before being sucked back into the dream where IT was waiting.

Packing in the morning was easy. I hadn't brought much with me, nor had I collected much during the six weeks on campus. Unlike other candidates, who were stuffing their suitcases with Princeton souvenirs, I was glad to leave IT behind. Forgetting the Princeton Experience was going to be as easy as packing. Like forgetting the so-called Black Experience. A few marches, some Afros, and the six o'clock news. It's the thing, gotta get a piece of it. Then it's over. So went the Princeton Experience. I got it. Milked it. I'm gone.

The only thing that I gained from being at Princeton was no sleep, a lot of grief, and a big question about higher education. Namely, who needs it? Certainly not anyone headed for the real world. Time after time, the real world affirmed that what I needed was solid experience, to wear my creases just so, and a balance of charm and intellect to distinguish myself from the pack. A piece of paper was not going to do that.

I had to admit, I was psyched in the beginning. I had never thought less than an Ivy League School. I looked the part, I had the smarts. In my mind I was Princeton picture-perfect. When my friends were talking Temple, Howard, and Syracuse, I had only to whisper "Princeton" to silence them.

Then I saw Mrs. Reeves, my college advisor, who agreed I was a Princeton man and said that she would do everything she could to get me in. It wasn't like she had to work hard. What college wouldn't want a class valedictorian? Colleges everywhere were throwing red carpets in my face. But she told my folks that she could get me into Princeton, as though twelve years of straight As and 98s had nothing to do with it. Then she looked at me. Really lay one deep like, "Okay, this is just you and me, kid," as though she had peeked my hole card. She said, "You have the makings, the ability . . . but you never use them fully, and that won't do."

Princeton came across, but would only admit me under some minority program. Even worse, my folks ignored the obvious insult and got sucked into Mrs. Reeves's "get everything you can" speech. Everything being six weeks of playing remedial catch-up. *Remedial?* How could you even open your mouth to say Denzel Watson, class valedictorian, Kid Whiz, and remedial all in the same sentence?

"I can't possibly qualify for this program. It's for academic underachievers," I protested while Mrs. Reeves inspected my financial aid forms.

"Don't think we didn't stretch it to get you in," she said, proud of herself. "Denzel, your SATs were not exactly competitive."

"What do you mean? I scored second highest in the school."

"But nationwide you're average."

That was that. If I wanted to get into Princeton, or any other Ivy League school, I was better off coming through a program that offered noncredit introductory courses for students from "under-enriched" educational backgrounds. Hence, the Princeton Experience.

For six weeks I put up with the humiliation of being a "candidate," as though I weren't a true and valid scholar. Candidate. It even sounded tentative, as if there were some chance I wouldn't make it.

The other candidates, like my roommate Arnold, didn't have the good sense to be insulted. Arnold, a proposed chem major from D.C., welcomed the sub-human treatment, forehead glistening, smile ever ready. He was always quoting success ratios of students from schools in affluent areas versus minority students coming from public schools. "Let's face it, Denzel. Twenty percent of our grades are for good conduct in a war zone, not academic ability. Our ninety-fives are equivalent to their seventy-fives," said he—something his college advisor must have told him during the "don't feel badly if you can't cut it" speech. What could I expect? Arnold was always full of it. If it wasn't that, it was "They're not smarter than us. Just better educated. Ready for this environment, whereas we're ready to be commended for being studious. There's a difference, my friend." It was no wonder that most of my class notes were doodles of Arnold Wells blowing off his head in a chem explosion with captions like "Oops! I'm inferior."

"You really believe that?" I asked the guy who scored highest on the math SATs in his district.

He smiled, nodded, and plowed through Chem notes that weren't even part of the summer program. He called it keeping up with the fall competition.

Six weeks of Arnold's smile and constant denial of his intelligence convinced me to never have another roommate—certainly not one who thought of himself as being beneath his abilities. After all, behaviors rub off. Anyone from the program was out of the question. They swallowed inferiority pills for breakfast. If I *were* coming back in the fall, I'd get a regular roommate—one who was as bright as I was and knew it.

From the beginning, I concluded that the whole point of The Program was to beat my manhood into submission. This occurred to me during my Intro to American Literature class as Dr. Wolthrop looked at us with his favorite *You shall succumb* glare. *Submit and be one with the other sheep who so easily denounce their intelligence. Rebel and be made an example of.* I was aware of all that psychological warfare. Make them doubt. Make them admit their faults. Make them bow.

Knowing the rules gave me immunity, and I was in a constant state of rebellion. My father would have been proud; my mother, apologetic. Having read me clearly, Wolthrop accepted the challenge and went after me. I would be the class example.

Wolthrop gave us one day to read one hundred pages of *On the Road* for the next class. He even told us what topics would be discussed, which, thought I, was a grave mistake, because unlike the rest of the class, I would be using my secret reading method—a method that not only got me through school but to the top of my class.

Step One: Learn all of the names of the characters in the book. Distinguish the protagonist from the minor characters. Find out what the protagonist's inner conflict is and how he resolves it (e.g., search for key words: *vex, conflict, struggle*). Step Two: Find the big thing—the flood, the death, the war, the locusts. Draw parallels between the big thing and the protagonist's inner conflict. Step Three: Be on the lookout for phrases that repeat from chapter to chapter. These are what's known as the big theme giveaways. Step Four: Key in on the dialogue to get a sense of the other characters. Always read dialogue with exclamation marks, or passages that look different—extracts, foreign words, all italics, and caps. Those are always on the tests. Then for back-up, read the Cliffs Notes.

I finished the hundred pages of *On the Road* in an hour and ten minutes, while Arnold plowed through the assignment word by word. As I was turning over in my sleep, Arnold continued with Calculus. I got up in the middle of the night to go to the bathroom and saw that lights were still on in the other candidates' rooms. They were sitting straight, spines flat against study chairs, books under desk lamps, believing every bit of the minority catch-up theory.

In the morning I came to class well rested and prepared, even feeling sorry for the other candidates, and vowed to share my secret method after they fell on their faces from lack of sleep. Once they saw my reading method in action they'd gladly pay for it, and I would establish a power base within the group, which would come in handy.

Dr. Wolthrop began the discourse. Instead of asking for a show of hands, he assumed that everyone had read the assigned pages of *On the Road*. Much to my surprise, he did not ask about the key occurrences. "What happened when" and "who said" were never mentioned. Instead, he began with a vague statement about "the purpose of an individual" and trailed off into "the rhythm of life as it related to the beatnik period," weaving in the use of the stream of consciousness technique. It got deeper. Hands shot up responding to remarks about beatnik art and cultural awakening. The entire class seemed to have input when he asked who were the artists and who were the impostors and what did each clique in the book represent in terms of a philosophical movement. While they jumped back and forth between art and intellect, I was still stuck on the beatniks. With my mind full of questions, my face a blank, I gulped when the Doctor blended my name into the discussion about Dean Moriarty, and waited for my answer.

Don't sweat it. Let them know that you at least know that Dean Moriarty is, in fact, a character in the book. So, I started with Dean's entrance and that he and Sal conversated on where they were going and the significance of going nowhere and how Sal was like salvation and Moriarty was like death and . . .

In the middle of my answer the professor's lips curled on the word *conversate*, and sure enough the word came back to haunt me. For in front of the other candidates, he wrote the word on the blackboard, separating the syllables, deriving the root words, and explained that *conversate* was vernacular, hardly a word for the university, and if such a nonword was ever found in a paper it would discredit the paper's entire contents.

He then disregarded the rest of my contribution about Moriarty's hitchhiking and picked up with another candidate who answered as I should have. He motioned for me to stay when the rest of the class was dismissed. His skinny finger beckoned me to the front. I felt it coming with every step I took toward him. *You shall succumb, Mr. Watson. You shall kneel before me and beg for mercy.*

With eyebrows raised and voice lowered, he kept his head down as though I were not worth the trouble of lifting his head to look at. "Mr. Watson, are you familiar with the principle of academic honor at Princeton?" Before I could say anything he answered, "Of course not." He cleared his throat, making way for the dreaded tongue-lashing. "We take academic honor very seriously here, Mr. Watson. Your honor speaks for your work. Your honor speaks of who you are." Then he looked up at me and said, "Who does that make you, Mr. Watson?" Another rhetorical question that was supposed to be crippling. "Mr. Watson, you are a dishonorable character. Sooner rather than later it will hang you. Until such time that the noose has choked you, do not ever come to my class unprepared. Are we at least clear on that?" No answer. "Good," he said, and went back to his notebook without actually saying "dismissed."

That was it. The meeting at his desk never went any further. I was free to tell my folks about it, or not. I didn't get any punishment from my counselor, who never heard about it. I received no memos on Princeton letterhead saying, "We expect better of you, Denzel." Just a slap on the wrist and a word or two about honor and being unprepared, like Wolthrop was doing me some grand favor. All in all, an easy acquittal.

How could I take any of it seriously? Even the program was based on the honor system. We were all accepted to Princeton whether we drew As or Fs. Whatever grades we got were strictly between us and the instructors. I mean, what was the purpose of sweating if there was to be no prize in the end?

Arnold remained amazed at my lack of concern but stopped praising my cavalier attitude.

There were other such incidents in Wolthrop's class: correcting my speech, banning my Cliffs Notes, prefacing my class remarks and papers with "Denzel, get to the point."

Intro to American Literature wasn't my only problem. Any class where I had to read, write, say, or solve something eluded my clever study methods. I began to think Wolthrop conspired with the other instructors to fail me. When I confided in Arnold he said, "Are you really that important?" Why did I think I could talk to Mr. Brown Nose?

When Arnold failed as a possible friend, I tried out Griffin, the counselor who was assigned to Arnold, me, and four other male candidates. Instead of understanding me he abused me with, "I got you read, brutha. We get one of you every year. Well-spoken chocolate chip cookies trying to skate through the program. Never make it beyond the second semester— which explains why there's a lot of well-spoken would-be's skating on what they coulda, shoulda been. Now, brutha, you still have a choice. You can either skate yourself on outta here with the rest of the would-be's or you can wake up, brutha. It's on you."

Everybody's on a power trip. I dismissed him.

"Arnold, higher education is for those who have to get up on a stepladder to reach the essence of their brain," I told my roommate after we got back our final marks at the end of the program. "Higher education is for those who have to be led. Higher education is a way station for people who don't know what to do with themselves."

Twelve o'clock was the official checkout time. I ate my last dining hall meal listening to promises to stick together no matter what, and to be eternal study partners.

A group of candidates had invited me to ride into Manhattan with them, but I had turned them down. I wished I hadn't. My father was picking me up and insisted on coming alone so we could talk man to man. If he really meant talk, as in a two-way exchange, that would be okay. But Vernon was Vernon, and it was going to be a long two hours.

One by one, the proud families came to collect their candidates and talk about big welcome-home dinners. I looked at Arnold and then at his parents. Arnold never had a prayer. The Einstein bifocals, the stupid smile, the shine on his forehead had been decided when X met Y chromosome. I forgave him his distorted views of higher education. He was descended from Mr. and Mrs. Egghead, and was proud of it.

Arnold shook my hand and said he'd see me in September. I knew he wouldn't and I believed he knew it also. The closer I was to getting out of there, the stronger my desire became to go to Queensborough or York Community College.

Finally the moment of dread came. My father drove up wearing a big shirt stuffed with the kind of pride that I found both embarrassing and stifling. I could see "Look at my son at Princeton" emblazoned on his chest as we shook hands.

I'd be okay as long as the old man didn't find another face from his generation. You know. The "right on" generation. The fist generation. Even worse, a former Students for Racial Equality compadre. As long as there was no one else that Pops could give his "we as a people" speech to, we'd be out of there in a heartbeat cruising along the New Jersey Turnpike.

That would have been *too* easy. We couldn't just leave quickly so I could erase Princeton from memory. No. The very second that I picked up my suitcase, Dad started complaining of hypertension and wanted to rest.

Aw, man. Had it been Lydia we'd have been flying past the New Jersey cornfields, homeward bound. I offered to drive back. Vernon chuckled and said "no way" like he was crushing a dream of mine. Now, had I been dreaming of a car, it would have been a sleek aerodynamic baby with some real horsepower—certainly not the conservative family auto.

Our departure was delayed another hour while he rested in the dorm.

Finally we were rolling. I tried to sleep in the car. Sooner or later he'd get me. I knew how Vernon's mind worked: *Let's turn the radio back to 1962 before R&B was diluted into sugar water. Let's segue into the war between saxes on the all-jazz station. Let's lecture on how young people are committing cultural genocide by distorting the music of our people. And then when Son starts to yawn, stretch, show some signs of life, let's run down every fear the missus and I could think of.*

There was no use fighting it. On the way home I endured questions and lectures on the ways of the white man, how to deal with injustice and jealousy, white girls looking for black studs, drugs, and skirt-chasing. I laughed at an appropriate pause—not at Dad's witty remark, but at both of my parents' overconcern for my genitals and how I was to be perceived by white people. What was I? So many pints of testosterone out of control? The ultimate ink spot taking a dip in white milk? Did Vernon and Lydia care as much for my legs, thumbs, and ears as they did for my genitals? I forgave them, seeing that they were strictly products of their generation; they could only see themselves as little black beings, and sex and the Peace Corps were all young people had to look forward to back then.

We were on the road at the worst possible time of day. The sun was at its highest point and Vernon was taking those deep breaths he used to calm himself when his blood pressure started to climb. He finally broke down and turned the wheel over to me about twenty miles into our ride. Not that he rested his jaw.

Traffic grew heavy as we came into New York. We sat in gridlock on the Verrazano Bridge while Charlie Parker's sax and Vernon Watson's lectures took turns bouncing on my eardrum. I could take the racket if we were mobile, but this standing still was getting to me. I had to do something about it. I searched my side and rear-view mirrors for the opening that would let me tear out and get the car rolling. I saw it. A break in the left lane. I put my foot down and tore left before the car to our left could inch up. A few more openings left and then right and we were cruising.

I knew my way home from the bridge, but Vernon spouted directions anyway. We took his way—the long way. Finally we were on the Van Wyck, which meant the Linden Boulevard exit was approaching and we'd be home in five minutes. The first thing I was going to do was lock myself in my room and not see anyone.

We were in Jamaica. It was like being welcomed back into the real world. While I was at Princeton honing useless skills, life continued to buzz where Linden met Merrick Boulevard. The Q85 ran north and south up Merrick. The Q84 split left up Linden. Mister Softee was pied-piping kids into ice cream fits. Basketballs were being hurled in St. Albans Park, five, six games at a time. The fellas were leaning against the Neighbor hood Superette to keep the building standing upright. People continued to move up and down the boulevards, while I had been sitting in a dorm room slam-dunking papers with red marks.

Except for Vernon's droning I was glad to be at the intersection waiting for the light to change. I looked over at the guys leaning against the Superette. Now these were some brothers who could benefit from Vernon's run-on lectures instead of yours truly. I knew better than to make that suggestion. Vernon Watson was nobody's hypocrite. He'd have had me pull the car over while he got out, slapped palms with the brothers, and gave them valuable information on clinics, counseling, and overcoming, which he kept in his glove compartment.

It was this behavior that made it impossible for Vernon Watson to pass the bar exam, accept a token job at a major fuel corporation that would not employ Blacks in South Africa, or attend Lydia's sorority functions, which he claimed fostered intraracial discrimination and only supported socially lukewarm but fashionable causes. We could have had everything and then some if Vernon would have just woken up. It wasn't as though his doing research and filing papers on field number 33 would take money out of some South African's hut.

Mom had her way of dealing with it.

So did I.

For Father's Day, when I was eight, I made a replica of an island with clay, buttons, matches, dried grass, and Popsicle sticks. I stuck a Black G.I. Joe soldier in the middle, made a red, black, and green flag, and put it all in a shoe box. I used black construction paper for water and erected a sign on a toothpick that said "Black air" and shoved the gift between him and his *Amsterdam News*. "Here," I exclaimed proudly after creating a perfect Black world for Vernon. Dad was in shock. I was in stitches. He couldn't see how a son of his could think that was funny or appropriate. Mom explained it in three words that only now have meaning: "The new seed."

The light changed. Dad had moved on to the good old days when "we" weren't allowed to say "Ivy League college," let alone attend one. He practically drooled. If Dad could have jumped back into 1962, he'd have been gone yesterday. "Just be aware of the new attack dog, son," he added as though he were really telling me something. I stopped short at the challenge and weighed things. On one hand, Vernon was a ridiculous dinosaur who couldn't bury a bone. On the other hand, Vernon could still kick my ass.

We rolled past the legendary house that was once owned by James Brown, and turned deep into the seclusion of Addesleigh Park. Addesleigh Park was a neat triangle of beige Tudor houses and Swiss chalets. The block association saw to it that every yard had a weeping willow tree, a lamp post, and matching garbage cans. Local politicians and celebrities lived in Addesleigh Park. I used to think we lived there because I was the smartest kid in Jamaica. I later learned the house was a gift to my mother from Vernon.

We pulled into the driveway. Dad said to go on inside while he got my suitcase. The door swung open before I could reach for the knob. To my horror, there was music playing, proud relatives in the living room, a feast cooking, and a six-foot banner that said in computer writing: WELCOME HOME DINIZULU. My sister, Kerri, jumped up and down like a puppy wanting approval for making the banner and using my given name. Only she and Vernon called me Dinizulu. The rest of the family had been relieved when I came up with my own version of the African name Dad had given me.

Six weeks had made a difference in my twelve-year-old sister. Kerri had become increasingly silly as her body matured. She wouldn't stand still long enough for me to hug her, so I gave her a noogie sandwich on her forehead.

Lydia came out of the kitchen and squeezed me, and then fluttered back to the kitchen. The rest of the maternal welcome was left to Nana Dee, who dragged out all of the old infantile nicknames. My flat top got raked and dented by aunts who had no respect for a guy's do. My uncles tried to slap twenty pounds off my back, like I could spare it. I got hugged, shaken, and blessed from all around the room when all I wanted to do was lock myself in my room, turn on the headphones, and fade away.

The only relief of the evening came from Nana Dee, who told Vernon to play something that the kids wanted to hear on the stereo "instead of that bebop horn slop," insulting his jazz collection. Dad turned up his nose going through my cassettes. Leave it to Nana Dee to speak her heart. I was glad when she moved in with us.

My cousin Randy showed up for a few minutes. Randy was going to Hofstra out on Long Island in the fall. He had just finished going through the same kind of program as I, and couldn't wait to get back in September. Before we could get into it he said he had to cut out. I couldn't blame him. It was too much family.

I could thank Lydia for suffocating me with wall-to-wall relatives. Any excuse to break out the china and do the hostess shuffle for the folks. Not only were there relatives in every corner of the house, but my prom date, Foxy Brown, stopped by. There she sat on the sofa going through a family album, giggling with my sister. It figured. My aunts would make it their business to investigate Foxy Brown.

After all of the family togetherness and ceremony wore down there was still no one in the room to talk to. I contemplated Dad, but he would have completely ignored me to bring it down to the white man's role and I wasn't in the mood.

I skipped Lydia. She pissed me off for having this family circus.

Randy was gone. Besides, we were too close, too competitive.

Kerri was anxious to talk to me, but I didn't want to be bothered. I didn't care how much Voltaire she read. Kerri was still a baby with no insight into the real world.

I looked at Foxy Brown, and Lydia's words briefly came back to haunt me. The girl lacked personality. In my mind, I had ended it when I took her home from the prom. Leave it to my folks—especially Lydia—to misunderstand, inviting her to my house as my girlfriend.

Then I looked at Nana Dee. We both went into the kitchen at the same time and it only seemed natural. I was her favorite. Firstborn grandchild. And she was quick to remind me that she used to change my diapers, knew the mess I could be. I sensed she wanted to talk to me, too, away from the family.

"Vern should be a lawyer with his own firm. Vern should be a good many things he ain't. Instead of fighting the world, he should be on top of it. Now, don't get me wrong. He's a good and strong man. But he don't never see nothing through. He don't live up to his potential and there's a world there. Just take note of what I'm saying. See this Princeton through," she said, almost knowing what I had to say. "You got a lot of Vern in you—yes you do," she teased, knowing that's one way to get me. "But you got other things too. Just don't let us down. Our hopes is in you, son."

"Well, Nana—"

"Hush, they comin'. Make like you're handing me that there," she said, pointing to the dishrag.

15

Lydia came in the kitchen and scolded Nana for washing dishes. Then she threw me back into center stage, where they were all waiting for the return of the son. It was my turn to get into the family spirit and start with my stories about how their shooting star had exploded all over Princeton, dazzling my professors with things I wasn't supposed to know. Who was I to tell them that I had no intention of going to Princeton in the fall? It was important to give them their day. Like the science fair medals. The speech and debate trophies. The Arista Awards Night. Junior and senior high valedictorianships. The 98.8. It gave credence to their own intelligence. They needed to display their son the brain.

They leaned forward, ready to caw, whoop, and holler at my version of *On the Road*. Midway into the first story, when the dessert tray was being wheeled out, I thought I would be sick.

GIRLS CAN'T BE KNIGHTS

I OPENED my eyes and put my hand over my heart. It was 7:15 A.M. and my heart was intact, beating smoothly. My palms and forehead were dry. I had slept six hours without ITs orange and black paw going for my face or heart.

I stretched, wiggled my toes, and yawned wide. I was almost home free. Not quite there. Pieces of my recurring dream started to flash in and out while I lay still on the bed. I could see frames of IT stalking the perimeter of my dream, looking for that opening. Frames of me fending IT off with a weapon that, at first, resembled a spear. As I became fully awake I realized the weapon was not a spear but my mind. Had to be my mind. Too sharp to be a stick.

I sat up. The solution came to me at once. I had to use my mind.

I always knew IT was in my mind. What I didn't know was that I put IT there. Fed IT. Kept IT alive by keeping IT inside. But now I was at home. In *my* room with *my* things. Not in a dorm room. Just the way I made IT big and lifelike, I could zap IT. Start slow. Say "Denzel, Princeton, and nosedive" in one breath.

The problem was finding the right set of ears to practice on before facing the folks. Someone whose world wouldn't crumble and who had nothing to gain by the knowledge that I could fail.

Nana Dee was my first choice. Once you had Nana you had the world. Vernon always deferred to his mother, and Lydia stayed out of Nana's way. When everyone else got excited over some award I had won, Nana always said, "You didn't exactly raise the dead." I'd grin back at her, wave my award, and stick out my tongue singing, "Na-na-na-Nana!" She never smacked me because she must have known one day I'd fall off my horse and come looking for her. But I had never thought Nana of all people would lay the family curse on me: *Our hopes is in you, son.*

My second choice would have been Randy. He and I could always talk as long as it was him doing the messing up. Randy was better at letting go of himself, whereas I maintained a scorecard. I was ahead because I made *Who's Who*. Then he won a Robeson Award. Cool. We both got into our colleges through the back door, but my college was Ivy League. *Slam-dunk on the rim.* I was going to live on campus while he commuted a hop, skip, and a bus stop to school. *Two points—mine!* Then my aunt and uncle bought Randy a hot new ride to commute in style. *Randy steals for the outside shot, putting the game into overtime. We both go for the lay-up.* I do my six weeks in the summer program, and he does his. *He nets Bs—swish! I die at the buzzer.*

I crossed Randy off the list.

There was my best friend.

She didn't always think I was so great, even though I out-ranked her point for point. But we could talk. We could get into it deep. The way she what if'ed and exhausted words, she'd have IT worked out of my system to the point that I could make jokes about IT. Then I could move on to Step Two: Facing the folks. Telling them that I was going to York Community College to be closer to home and save them money.

Only, there was this slight problem with Step One. The night before our senior prom my best friend had yelled, "I hate you, Denzel Watson," loud enough for all of Jamaica to hear, and hadn't spoken to me since.

Now I admit, it was a cold thing to do, dumping her thirty-six hours before the prom to take this other girl. But you had to see the other girl to understand. Even if *she* thought about it, weighed the obvious, she'd have to say, "No question. You did the only thing possible." But knowing my friend, she hadn't reached the point of taking it in stride, snapping on my white tux to make me laugh and know things were right between us. No. My best friend, Wendy Kilpatrick, would probably pick now to come across like a true female and withhold the things I needed most to make me feel better—her presence and her silence.

I got out of bed. Lydia would be leaving for work in the next fifteen minutes. If I wasn't up, she would see to it that I was. She had this thing about us being in bed past seven-thirty. The only one allowed to sleep long was Nana Dee. Otherwise, there was no lounging in pajamas in Lydia's house. It was get up. Get showered. Get dressed. Eat. Take your list of chores from the bulletin board. Then free time.

I selected my clothes for the day and showered.

As always, the patter of computer keys was coming from Kerri's room. I stuck my head inside to say hi. Being away for six weeks made things that had dulled with familiarity sharp and noticeable. Her room hadn't changed in the ten years that we lived in the house. Those red bow ties scattered on her bedroom wall belonged to gingerbread men that had faded into the beige wallpaper. Her collection of blue-black dolls (gifts from Vernon) still sat on the windowsill keeping a vigil over her princess bed. Her library spilled out of her bookcase onto the floor in stacks. Most of those books I recognized— not because I had read them but because they were originally mine and were passed on to Kerri. They were gifts from Vernon and Lydia, or from teachers who thought I would appreciate them. After a while I learned to flip through the pages for quiz purposes, then placed them on Kerri's shelf where I knew they would be read from preface to epilogue.

A tune played merrily on the computer. Kerri was so pleased with herself that she didn't know I was standing in the room shaking my head. Six years from now she'll still be sitting in her gingerbread room playing computer games, I thought.

"Hey, big head."

She turned around and smiled. Even her teeth were baby teeth.

"You should talk, Dinizulu. You and Daddy have melon heads."

"I'd worry, little sis. It's hereditary." I put my arm around her neck. She squirmed away.

The computer beeped.

"See! You messed me up!" she complained.

"Computer games, Kerri?"

"Homework." She tried to look annoyed, but underneath it she was only too happy to tell me about it. "See? I programmed this game, RUN RABBIT RUN, using my own binary language. If the hunters catch the rabbit then the computer plays the Death March and the game's over. But if the rabbit gets past the snares, outruns the hunters, and escapes down a burrow, it plays the theme from *Dr. Zhivago* and advances to the next screen. Neat, huh?"

"Little sis, you need some sunlight."

I went downstairs. Dad was in the kitchen. He didn't have to be at work until nine-thirty, which gave him enough time to drive Kerri to computer camp.

"Morning, Dad."

"Son."

I waited the appropriate two minutes while he read an article. I sensed he was at a stopping point and now was a good time to approach. Banzai.

"Guilt's a killer, Dad."

"What's it all about, son?"

I knew I was going to regret this conversation long before it started. But Dad was there. Purposely there, sipping coffee with a blank stare, ready to climb inside my head, and I needed to talk to someone.

"I took the wrong girl to the prom. Should have been Wendy."

He drank his coffee as though I had said nothing. I knew he wouldn't understand and would think something was wrong with me for caring. It was more than not taking the right girl. Wendy Kilpatrick and I had been friends through kindergarten, eight years of special classes, and four years of honors. I talked her into running as VP under me, knowing she wanted to run for class president—and we were still friends. When I beat her out of being valedictorian by an eighth of a point and she called me "an incredibly lucky bum whose luck would run out," we were still friends.

Had Wendy been Black, Dad would have lectured me about respecting sisters and about the evils of gaming. But Wendy Kilpatrick was unmistakably white, undeniably Irish, and not about to apologize for either fact, even if she was one of a handful of whites who attended the school.

Wendy rated a halfhearted "Is that all?" from Vernon.

"No, Dad. That's only the beginning," I said, embarking on a useless explanation of who Wendy was to me.

"That Debra's a nice girl," Dad said in Foxy's defense. "Good family. And if you ask me, much better looking. But if you want to stew over some white girl, do it elsewhere. I'm having breakfast."

"Dad, after twelve years of us building science projects in this kitchen, *all* you saw was Wendy's color?"

"Non-color."

"I'm serious and you're making jokes." A good sign if I wanted to continue this conversation. "Didn't you ever know someone who was more than their non-color—as you put it?"

Dad set his green mug down, letting it clack hard against the table as though that were part of his answer. A smirk crossed his lips. I already regretted this. He turned to see if Lydia was around. "One," he answered.

"What was she like?"

"Like? She was beautiful! Blonde hair, blue eyes. You know the look."

What I knew was how fruitless this was. We were a world apart, as my mother had implied when she called me the "new seed."

"Seriously Dad, what was she like?"

The gap between us became apparent when he grunted. He was annoyed with me, because in his mind he had already answered my question.

"What d'ya mean, son?"

22

"I mean, was she a nice person? Was she funny? What did she like to do? Those kind of things. Was she easy to talk to?"

"Talk?"

"Yeah. Talk."

Dad might as well have spat. "She went to jail for me," he boasted. "That's the kind of girl she was." He looked around to see where Lydia was before going on. "This was back in the days when I headed cultural affairs in school. I got Malcolm X to be a guest speaker on campus. Well, once the school administration got wind of it they revoked our assembly permit. Heh, heh. That was supposed to stop me.

"She'd see me waiting outside the dean's office with my petitions. Was dying to talk to me, let me know she was sympathetic to the cause. Want to know just how sympathetic? Handcuffed herself to a tree in the dean's garden to protest the ban on Malcolm X. She did that just after we made it."

On cue, Lydia came out, briefcase in hand, ready to go to work. "Honey, please. Let that poor gal rest some." Mom tapped me on the shoulder, smacked down a list of busy work in front of me, and smiled pathetically at Dad. She went out the front door, apparently unruffled by my father's fling with the white girl. Dad shot me one of those "She's a woman, what d'ya expect?" glances, but I could read my mother's lack of concern. The girl happened yea decades ago, and was nothing more than a revolutionary sacrifice to my father, who was then looking for yet another means of getting back at "honky." He didn't know that girl any more than he knew what I was talking about. Deep conversation between Vernon and me had never existed before. Why I thought it might at 7:35 on a Monday morning was sheer foolishness on my part.

Dad called upstairs telling Kerri to move it.

Granted, I was never in love with any of the girls I pursued and eventually got over on. I just liked their way of saying no when they meant "How high will ya jump, Jack?" I might not have loved them, but I didn't know what it was to screw the enemy. And as sure as Dad couldn't remember the girl's name, she was "them" to him—enemy conquest.

Wendy wasn't a them. Wendy was a girl with wild red hair and no fashion sense, who was my academic rival since kindergarten.

The student body expected me to take Wendy to the prom. Prez and VP. Valedictorian and salutatorian. Captain and cocaptain of the debate team. When were we not together? She even asked me to break her in so she would know what it was like. I did. She said, "Oh," and that was that. No heavy discussion. Nothing bitter behind it. Just two friends helping each other out. In that way, Wendy was an all right guy.

Even *I* knew I shouldn't have blown that. Girls don't know how to be friends. They can't even be friends with each other. They put conditions on everything and try to hold you to them. Girls can't be knights. They don't know the code.

Wendy came close though. This close. The first sign of rain, she reverted into a she-thing who finds hidden meaning in "later," gets hysterical when it's least needed or expected, and mad 'cause you can't figure out what it is that she wants.

The really simple girls want a remembrance. A gold bracelet, a son, or something like that. Wendy didn't want a trinket. She wanted me to take her to the prom, a neat finish to twelve years of friendship. We said we would keep in touch, but we both knew we were going our separate ways.

I wanted to leave things on good terms, too, but I also wanted something out of the prom. I planned. I sacrificed. I took a job at a car wash to pay for the tux, limo, and corsage. I gave up grease for months so my skin would stay clear. I turned down girls who were giving up a quick one behind the handball court, just to avoid any misunderstanding. I narrowed down my "A" list. Made it a point to keep a casual conversation going with the girls on my list so I wouldn't disqualify myself because *"you didn't say hello to me in home-room for a whole seven months so who do you think you are, asking me to the prom?"*

The SATs didn't get as much preparation as prom night. Even for us, the ultra sublime, prom night is special. As corny as we outwardly say it is, we believe in its magic. The meanest dudes and the tackiest girls come clean for prom night. Doors open, arms are offered, seats are held out, and girls give you the magical feeling that something wonderful is about to happen even if it isn't. Or they at least have the courtesy to suspend the magic before saying, "Okay, but don't mess up my dress."

Just for the moment when every head turns, and the music almost stops because you walk in with her, there is prom magic. The more I visualized this magic, the more I regretted promising to be Wendy's escort.

I made my first mistake by telling her sophomore year that I would take her to the prom. Why? Because it was almost three years away and the feeling of the prom hadn't even occurred to me. Then I did it again in our junior year, promising to take her if she wasn't seeing anyone who would mind. Senior year I sort of said the same thing out of habit and then June came and I didn't want to take her. Besides, all of my options with other girls were peaking and it just seemed like a waste to do something I *should* do over something that I *wanted* to do. Suddenly I was in demand. Girls knew the kind of stories a prom photo with me would give them for their grandchildren: "I didn't go with just anyone. He was class valedictorian, senior president . . ."

The more I thought about it the more I began to feel Wendy

just wasn't special enough to take to the prom. It wasn't like I wouldn't dance with her, or take a picture with her. We could share a table. She could ride in my limo.

She just couldn't be my main girl for the evening. Wendy was okay in every other way, but she just didn't complete the picture in my dreamscape. The girl who did was named Debra Jordan, although we all called her Foxy Brown. Foxy tried to act like she didn't like the name, but we knew she did. One day there she was, standing at the bus stop on Francis Lewis Boulevard waiting for the Q76 as though my thinking of her had put her there. Now, there was only one reason why someone like Foxy would smile pitifully and make conversation about beautiful June weather. She must have had a quarrel with her boyfriend, which left her without a date for the prom. It would have been rude to leave Foxy hanging, so I did what I thought was the right thing at the time.

Only, it backfired. Wendy didn't get over it like I anticipated. Her face turned to stone at commencement. She wouldn't shake my hand, applaud my speech, or acknowledge me during the ceremony.

Now the shoe was on the other foot. I needed her friendship, and she could either come through or crush me like a roach.

The list of chores that Lydia left me only occupied me for a little while, and gave me too much space to think about things I would eventually have to say to Wendy. Around nine I locked up and started walking to Wendy's house, twenty-three blocks down Linden. By the time I got there I would have it all ready. A neat apology that would get over without having to crawl. I hated having to do this. Apologize. Talk soap. But the fact remained: If I had taken Wendy to the prom, I'd now have someone I could talk to. Even the can I kicked down the street rambled on in enough tin syllables to say *Denzel, you're a wrong dude.*

The Kilpatricks had been living in the brown house on 198th Street and 116th Avenue as far back as "when the neighborhood was still nice," which was Mrs. Kilpatrick's way of putting it. Mrs. Kilpatrick lived in that neighborhood as a little girl. She attended Andrew Jackson along with a class full of Young White Americans flanking her in her *Pioneer* yearbook. As the neighborhood steadily lost its "niceness" and the faces in Andrew Jackson's yearbook became progressively darker, whites began to leave St. Albans and Hollis. Most retreated to the border where Queens Village met Long Island. Others fled Queens altogether and headed for Ronkonkoma, Connecticut, or Utah. If the neighborhood wore down to a crime-infested frazzle, Mrs. Kilpatrick would just build her fence a little higher, put more rose hedges in her front yard, and keep on pruning. No one was going to move Mrs. Kilpatrick. Even after Wendy's dad, a police officer, was gunned down in the candy store around the corner, Mrs. Kilpatrick wouldn't budge from her house on 198th Street.

I made my mother take me to their house to pay our respects. Mrs. Kilpatrick slapped the gladiolus out of my hand and said, "We don't want your damned flowers." My hand stung, and so did my pride, but I was still Wendy's friend. Lydia yanked me from the porch screaming "see!" and we drove home, where Lydia got play-by-play hysterical in front of Vernon, who wasn't above storming the widow's house with members from the Black Just-US League, demanding restitution and "just-us" for my gladiolus.

Would Wendy remember how I let her cry and snot up my silk designer shirt when they told her her father was dead? Would she remember how I always walked her home the long way, looping around 198th and Linden so she wouldn't have to see the candy store where her father was shot? Would she remember that I had been her friend too?

I stood at her porch. My hand got warm as I rang the doorbell. Mrs. Kilpatrick opened the door. She was wearing a loose housedress that had been washed one too many times. She was a large, intimidating woman, who, like Wendy, didn't put much into styling her hair; she just wore it loose, parted in the middle, except hers had a little gray on the sides. Her lips were thin and dry. Her emerald eyes had no humor. All I could think was *Is that what Wendy is going to look like twenty years from now? Egaadz.*

"Thought you were away at school." In other words, why are you here? Haven't you done enough?

"That was just freshman orientation," I chose to call it. Sounded a lot better than minority program. Orientation was more general, blanketing all freshmen. Minority program was like the welfare stamp that they put on government surplus food.

"Come in. I'll tell Wendy you're here."

I looked around the living room for the picture that hung in both the Kilpatrick living room and ours. It was a picture of our kindergarten class at the crosswalk, which appeared on the cover of the magazine section in the Sunday paper. The focus was on our hands leading our class. At the time, we didn't know it was a significant picture. We thought it was just pretty, and that we were special because we were class leaders. It took twelve years to figure out that it wasn't a picture of Wendy and me, but the color of our joined hands with the caption "Is Integration Working?"

Wendy came down the stairs wearing one of those tee shirts I was sure she'd wear to the prom.

Actually, that night she surprised me by showing up at the prom with a guy who had nothing to do with Andrew Jackson, someone I didn't know. Wendy looked different that night. Nice. Very nice. She wore a green satin dress that looked great with her red hair. Her dress wasn't hot, like Foxy Brown's black mini dress, but Wendy looked special. Her hair was pinned up and the front was even curled. When I tried to tell her how nice she looked she turned away so I left it at that. I hadn't seen Wendy since we picked up our diplomas.

I knew I was staring. She had her hair cut short and it took me a second to place her round face, greenish eyes, and vanishing freckles under the short pageboy.

"So you're back," she said. "How was it?"

"Okay."

"Just okay? What? No fantastic tales about the brilliant Denzel Watson?"

"It was just okay. Not what I expected." I sat down on the sofa, waiting for her to sit. She stood.

"When do you go to Brown?" I asked.

"Last week in August." She finally sat down, which made me feel better. "So why are you here?" A question her mother only asked with her face.

"I need to talk to you."

"What about?"

"A few things, Wendy. First," I said, drawing in a deep breath, "I just want to tell you that I'm sorry for what went down."

"You mean that stupid prom?"

Her lips pressed tight with well-saved anger. It was like she hadn't moved since the day I told her I was taking someone else.

"Yeah. It was kinda cold. I know it was. I always said we'd go together and then I backed out. I don't even know why. I just did."

"Now who's kidding who?"

I looked down, then back up at her. Counted to two. She was getting on my nerves. I mean, here I was apologizing. "Hey, look. I came by to talk to you, friend to friend. You raggin' or what?"

"Friend to friend?" She started waving her arms like she was going to take off. "Denzel, friendship is convenient for you when it's good for something. What happened to friendship when I was stuck one day before the prom without an escort? I would have gone with someone else but you *asked* me to go to the prom, friend. You made a big deal about how it was a perfect end to our friendship before going away to school."

I decided to be cool. I could spare it. Besides, she must have been rehearsing this all summer. Let her get her stuff off. Sit back and let her finish.

"You know what I think? I think you wanted to take me out to get at your old man, and then you chickened out."

I almost laughed because that wasn't it.

"My father had nothing to do with why I asked you," I told her although there was some truth in her accusation. "I asked you because you're my closest friend and you happen to be a girl."

"Lucky me."

Before all of this had started I could have told her I had dumped her because I wanted to take a showstopper, not my cut buddy from the sandbox days. But Wendy was now one of them—female with a vengeance.

"I had my reasons for backing out. They weren't good, I know that. But it's done and I'm sorry. What do you want?"

Wendy sighed like she had given up on me.

"Denzel, what do *you* want?" she asked.

"Nothing. Just to talk. See how you're doing. Let you know that I was sorry."

She nodded. Not with understanding but with momentary acceptance. "So talk," she said, moving away from the prom.

"It didn't go well, Wendy."

"What?"

"Princeton," I said. "Wendy, I went down in smoke. That's how bad it was. If I got a C I was doing okay and that's not the half of it," I said, glad to finally unload it on Wendy.

Wendy grinned at me. All of the humor that was missing in her mother's eyes was shining bright in Wendy's. "What happened? Found out you're not half the brain you thought you were? I always knew it would happen." She laughed and shook her head from side to side like she forgot she no longer had shoulder-length hair. "If you can't compete in a special program, how do you think you'll do against the academic elite?"

"Thanks for understanding." I got up to leave. It was pointless. She was still at the prom or on the rag.

"Understand? I understand far better than you think. I understand what it's like to be in the great Denzel's shadow for twelve years because I'm white and you're Black."

"What are you talking about?"

"Me. That's what I'm talking about. I was supposed to be valedictorian. *I* was. Not you. Add up your exams and papers against mine. We got the same grades, Denzel. The same. But they gave you an eighth of a point over me because the parents would raise the roof if they gave it to me, a white girl. Sure. You're more charismatic. But I always worked harder. I gave correct answers while you were being credited for dressing it up with your big words and your big talk. I resented how teachers patted you on the head while I busted my butt night and day. But I'm not worried. They did me a favor. I know I can go to Brown, put my nose to the grindstone, and get decent grades. Can you?"

"Wendy, you got to be kidding me. I never thought this was about jealousy."

"I *was* jealous. I *was* angry. Not anymore." Wendy's voice was now burden free. "I'm glad the real world found you out, Denzel. What a perfect graduation."

"Wendy, I thought you were better than this. I thought you were a friend. I take back my apology. I'm glad I didn't take you to the prom."

"Hah! You owed me the prom at the very least."

"Owed you the prom?" Did she know how stupid she sounded? Like a white girl.

She moved closer. We were standing eye to eye and she stuck out her finger, jabbed it into my chest, and yelled, "You owed me the prom and a whole lot more."

I would have punched her if she dug her finger in my chest one more time. I moved her hand away.

"Back off, Wendy. Just back off," I warned.

"You owed me," she kept saying as though I were supposed to know what she was talking about.

"For what? What did you do for me that was so great?"

Wendy's eyes became wild like she was going to jump on me. Mrs. Kilpatrick came out shouting that she kept her husband's revolver loaded. No argument there. I was gone.

FAST TALK ON A SLOW TRACK

*S*HE *was lying.*
I got on the bus and went home.
My marks were always higher than hers.
Lying.

I went upstairs to my room, dragged out my trunk from the closet, opened it, and started tearing through the twelve years of paper: tests, book reports, report cards. Nothing lower than an A minus. Big A pluses. Gold stars from first grade. "Excellents" from the third grade. "Outstanding" all throughout.

While the rest of my first grade class was spelling b-e-a-r I was writing essays. Look at that. *Carnivorous.* Used correctly. Spelled correctly. Outstanding!

Fourth grade. My favorite paper, "The Knights of the Round Table." Bibliography. Footnotes. Words that even the teacher didn't know. Ninety-nine.

Damn. Liquid *does* disintegrate twelve-year-old paper. I wiped my eyes and read my teachers' comments, studying their handwriting for false praise. There was not one mention of me needing to apply myself, be concise, or do anything else I was told at Princeton.

Instead, I found what I should have known all along. I was the best student that Andrew Jackson and J.H.S. 192 had to offer. My tests and reports confirmed that I had a mind for math, sciences, and historical facts, and could include words in an essay that only a scholar would use.

I felt stupid. How could I let Wendy get under my skin? Tell me something that couldn't possibly be true and then believe her? For that matter, how could I allow those six weeks at Princeton to have me running in circles, screaming in the middle of the night? Hadn't Vernon always said the world was full of jealousy and obstacles for truly bright people, and that I had better learn to recognize that fact and deal with it? Wasn't Princeton an obstacle that was supposed to stop me? Didn't Wendy turn out to be one jealous person? Weren't they all part of IT, the thing that made me lose control, made me doubt myself?

I hated to admit it but Vernon was right. Recognizing the game being played gave me control. Now I could deal with IT. Start putting things back in order.

I stacked all of the education I ever needed in three piles, and put my feet up and leaned back, digging my intelligence.

Bring on another nightmare! Bring on Princeton.

Even better—skip Princeton. Why fall into an obvious trap? Go to York Community. They accepted me without an application. I'd major in Business. Get straight As. Be out in three years, two and a half if I really pushed. In the end all the real world wants to know is if you have a piece of paper, not how much Daddy paid for it.

Or, forget college. Trim all the academic fat. Go directly to business school—the ones posted in subways. Be out with certificate in hand in six months. Set my sights on Wall Street. Redefine corporate takeover. In the real world they look for experience over paper anytime.

Of course, I would have to tell my folks my decision not to enter Princeton in the fall. I wouldn't spring it on them all at once, but I'd tell them eventually. Sure, there'd be static at first. A lot of blackmail about sacrifice from Lydia, and about debt to the Black community from Vernon. But I would wear them down with their own words about doing the right thing and making life's decisions.

Besides, I'd always stayed on the right track when the crowd said turn left. Vernon never had to go to court for me. Lydia wasn't made a granny before her time. They never found criminal evidence in my sock drawer.

At a lot of personal risk, I was a "goody." I mowed the lawn. Did my chores without slacking. Got straight As, my name in the paper for awards, and always gave them a reason to say "my son, my son." Now it was time to channel myself in my own direction. They'd have to understand.

Once my decision was out in the open and the hurricane died down, the folks would see that I made the best decision, sparing them a lot of financial burden and possible embarrassment. And in the end, I would wind up where Princeton was supposed to take me. I'd just get there sooner my way.

The day was wasting and I was sitting in my room. Something was wrong with that picture. I had to make a move, but where? I could find some people to be with, but my crowd was strictly college bound. Too hyped up on fall wardrobe, hooking up dorm rooms, and making dean's list first semester.

I wanted to get back into things, have some fun, but with

the right people. People who didn't know me as the smartest person on the planet. I had to get out of Addesleigh Park.

My first mistake was leaving through the back door without looking out the window.

"I see you're home, son."

It was Mr. Randall on his hands and knees, surveying his lawn. He had the world's bluest and neatest lawn. As soon as the grass thought about leaning left he was there to clip it right. He was like that with everything. Even his son, Morris.

He got up and waved me over with his clippers.

"Hello, Mr. Randall."

We shook hands. When he didn't have his teeth in, like now, Randall looked like a brown Jiminy Cricket in a tan fishing cap and gardening gloves. He had high, puffy cheeks, a narrow jaw, and hands that flew out from his body without warning, which was dangerous considering he was holding long, pointed clippers.

He started licking his thin lips and exercising his jaw— which meant only one thing. He wanted to talk. "I'm sure you can't wait to get back to school. Oh, I know you college boys. Frat man myself. When you're ready to choose a frat, see me. I'll steer you right."

"Thank you, sir. Well, I have to be going."

"Yah, son!" he said, clamping down on my shoulder with one hand. "Dem college days are fun . . . Parties, song and step shows, homecomings. Just don't get sidetracked by all of the partying. That's where you freshmen go wrong. Gettin' happy 'cause Mom and Pop aren't checking the homework. Now, take Morris . . ."

Here we go, I thought. Morris Randall was six years older than I, had graduated from Duke early and in the top percentile of his class, and had just finished law school at NYU. The last thing I wanted to hear was the Morris Randall story. Every move I made to get away from Randall was ignored.

"Well, give Morris my best. I'm sorry, Mr. Randall. I'm late for an interview."

"Interview? What? For a job?"

I jumped back to dodge a finger in the eye.

"Why you want to do that in your last four weeks of freedom? You should be sitting back, resting up for college."

"I know. I just can't seem to sit for too long. Know what Mom says about idle hands. Anyway, nice seeing you, sir," I said, walking away. Randall was still advising me on how to spend the rest of a summer that I had already planned.

First I had to take a bus, then hop on the E train to Jackson Heights, and reclaim my summer job. It was a gig I had stumbled onto as a joke with my cousin Randy, going door to door selling peanut brittle and cookies. The ad had called for sales trainees wishing to earn marketing experience. We had gone dressed impressively, full of hope, with our typewritten resumes. Randy wanted to turn around when he saw what the job really entailed—carrying a two-by-four case of cookies and candy door to door, giving a pitch. I convinced him to try it. Do a day's work as a joke, another chapter in the exciting lives of Randy and Denzel. After carrying a box all day and getting doors closed in his face, Randy dropped his cardboard case and got on the train with the two dollars from the one box of cookies he had sold. I couldn't go. There was this dude named Carmello, who had everyone awestruck, and I wanted to dethrone him. The prospect of beating out Carmello for the High Man bonus got me hooked. He was a true competitor. Nothing fazed him, which was good because I lived to keep him in the number-two slot.

The crews usually left after noon. I had to hurry if I was going to make Weber's crew. I got off the train at Roosevelt

Avenue in Jackson Heights, eager to see if my summer job was still waiting for me. Of course it was. They couldn't have the Summer Action Program without me. Jack, the sales manager, had even called my house before I left for Princeton, hoping I'd change my mind about not working the summer.

My folks didn't approve of my going door to door. They had both offered me work at their offices, but I couldn't see being with Lydia or Vernon for eight hours of work and then at home. What they had really wanted to do was put me on display for their coworkers. *Speak, son. Be Afro-American Intelligence at its best, son. Blow honky's mind, son.* The last thing they wanted to do was let it be known that I was selling cookies and candy. It wasn't dignified. It wasn't brag worthy. But I liked it. I was good at selling. Getting the door open. Reading the customers' faces. Knowing which pitch would work. Selling to diabetics and koshers. Stealing High Man away from Mello.

It was a few minutes after twelve. The office was three blocks from the subway. I could see Weber loading up his van. I wondered if he had the same old crew.

The office was one floor above a barber shop in a block of stores. I ran up the stairs, all the while listening to hear if the van was pulling off. When I got upstairs I scanned the outer office where the crews usually sat on benches waiting to go out. I didn't recognize any of their faces, but I knew the look. Happy to sit there. Hoping not to go out and sell.

I swung open the door to Jack's office. I must have surprised him because his coffee almost went in his face and the greasy shrimp-boat carton fell in his lap.

"I'm back," I said, out of breath.

Jack swallowed his coffee and coughed. He used his shirt as a napkin for the ketchup on his fingers. Jack was one sloppy human being. Always stuffing his face. Never buttoned his shirt over his belly. But he could laugh like a jolly Santa because he counted the money.

"So you are."

"Put me with Mello," I said.

"No go, kid. Van's loaded and ready to move." He looked at his roster. "Dave's carrying a light load. Got a fresh bunch of kids. They could benefit from seeing a master at work." He pushed back his belly to open the top drawer of his desk, took out a stack of orange cards, and dealt me a clean one.

"What do I look like? A tutor? Throw me with Mello and I'll come back High Man. Three cases easy."

Jack slurped some coffee and mulled it over. Who was he kidding? He was greedy. Besides, he knew what I could do when I was motivated.

"Blue van on the corner. Catch 'em before they pull off. Tell Lizzie Chiu to go with Dave's group."

I quickly scribbled my name on the card.

"So who will you be this time?" he asked.

"I tink I be Dinizulu. Foreign exchange student from Zululand, saving my people from de flood or de famine."

Dinizulu didn't exactly spring from my imagination. Dinizulu was my father's contribution to my eternal embarrassment. An African name. All because it was the thing to do at the time. Everyone was tracing their "roots," looking for their tribes, and changing their names. Now, I ask you. If I went back to Zululand and found my long lost cousins, would they say welcome? All this to thwart the establishment, shock Nana Dee into an early heart attack, and embarrass me, his only son. Did Dad change his name? No. He was still Vernon Everett Watson.

Kerri was lucky. When she was born the roots syndrome had died.

I, on the other hand, was stuck with Dinizulu until I was

nine. Vernon took me to see "When the Chickens Come Home To Roost," a play about the confrontation between Elijah Muhammed and Malcolm X. While Dad "rapped" with one of his "brothers," I read the playbill and came across the name "Denzel Washington," who was playing Malcolm X. Denzel. Denzel. I couldn't stop saying it. What a name. Like something flying fast down the train tracks. I was determined to have that name. I used psychology. I nagged my pops to take me to see the play with that dude "Denzel" who played Malcolm X. I wore Vernon out with praises of "Denzel, that guy who played Malcolm X," and how I wanted to be like him, and hey . . . even our names are alike. Then I started to call myself "Denzel, like the guy who played Malcolm X," which was a relief to the relatives who all called me son. Anything but Dinizulu. Except for Kerri, whose first clear word was not *Mama, Dada, doo doo,* or *baba,* but *Dinizulu.*

Sometimes it paid to be Dinizulu. Sometimes it didn't. I clipped my badge onto my lapel deciding today was payday.

I heard the engine turning over. I ran downstairs into the street to catch the van before it left. Luckily, Weber was backing up and saw me in the rearview mirror.

"Money man," he called out the window.

"That's me," I said, running up to the van. I leaned down to get a look inside. "Jack says the girl goes with Dave's crew." Lizzie Chiu was hugged up with Carmello and was not pleased. She kicked me on her way out of the van.

Carmello's face sank into his large hands. He cursed and stuck his palm out to me for the slap. He cursed again.

"Let the games begin," I said, accepting his welcome.

Metal clicked. Swords crossed tip to tip and slashed apart. It was going to be a great summer. His style versus mine.

I was sales perfection. Meticulous. Methodical. Could talk a dieter's no-sale into a "good conscience" double order. You see me, you see success, polish, background. A face you can trust for two dollars.

Mello was all wrong for the job, and it got him over every time. From the first glance through a screen door, he was intimidating. Questionably dressed. Slow mouthed. Probably had a nickel on a dollar scale of rap, which did not hurt his pitch. Mello was some kind of Latin mixed with some kind of "other," and girls of all persuasions loved him on sight and would die just to hear him say "so what." To watch them swoon and describe him, he was a bronze god—tall like a statue, with muscles like Adonis, and a face designed to get over.

If you stood us together, you had Clark Kent in Superman's shadow. We could dig each other and not dig each other because we had this code, a tacit agreement. I didn't push the *Encyclopaedia Britannica* down his throat; he didn't challenge me to benchpressing a building. Our code made us sterling knights. Abide by the code and everyone had a kingdom.

We headed out of Queens in the van. It was great to be back. I was flooded. Happy. Stupid. Blowing my cool. The things that had bothered me a while ago got pushed back to where I couldn't think about them. The only thing I could focus on was beating Mello. I couldn't wait to start selling.

Our territory was Brooklyn, which made sense. There was less of a chance of running into people who knew us because we were all from Queens. Brooklyn was full of high-selling areas with long blocks to canvas. We mainly worked Sheepshead Bay, Brooklyn Heights, and Park Slope. Weber made sure we worked a good area, and if the area went stale, he got us out and onto a new spot.

We cruised down around East 23rd Street and Ocean Avenue. Weber decided that this was going to be our first stop and began his usual summation of the area. "There's money to be made here. Good section. Lots of housewives. Lots of opportunities." He beamed. "If all goes well, we can work this area for the week. Be at your best. No going inside. No arguing with the customers. We don't want trouble." He looked in the rearview mirror at Shawanda. "Stick close to your partner. And *no*, absolutely *no* donations. Get it?"

He wasn't talking to Mello or me. We wouldn't sell if there were no fringes involved. We were both about profit and would raise the price by fifty cents or whatever we could get away with. Only a complete dunce would sell at a straight-up two bills. The others got Weber's drift, though. Robert, alias Bad, as in Bad Area Bob, cowered in his seat. His partner, Shawanda, folded her arms and muttered something that Weber wasn't supposed to hear but so what if he did. Mikie, the team mascot, saluted and said, "Right, chief."

"All right. This looks like a good spot," Weber said, parking the van. "Your pick-up point is Avenue I. That's eight blocks down. I'll be around to see how you're doing. Let's pitch 'em, sell 'em, thank 'em, and sell 'em again."

Mikie was dropped off first on Bay Street.

Mikie never had a bad day. He was consistent. Always worked alone. Always sold one case. Didn't care how many he sold after that and wasn't in on the quest for High Man. He just had to sell his one case. Once Mikie sold only fifteen cans and had one can of Nutty Crunch left. On the way back to Queens he carried on until Weber got off the highway and pulled into a street so Mikie could sell the lousy can.

Mikie got over with his cuteness. You couldn't slam a door on anything as cute and nonthreatening as Mikie. He didn't clear five feet, and my guess was he never would. He could make his voice sound like a ten-year-old's. He had absolutely no facial hair, and his skin was dewy reddish-brown. His head was covered with curly infant hair, and he had long, curly lashes. When he gave you his pitch you never knew he was on the downhill side of eighteen.

Bad and Shawanda were dropped off next. They never had to say they were from Liberty Avenue. They wore it. Sweat suits, suede sneakers in the summer, and a pound of gold between them. Hers was four gold battering rams threaded through each ear. His was an eighteen-karat gold rope and dog plate around his neck. As much as they complained about each other, they wouldn't switch partners, which was okay because who in his right mind wanted to work with either of them?

Shawanda was the schoolgirl bully who hadn't grown up beyond girl-ganging and proving she could hang like the fellas. Whatever looks she had were dragged down by her bulldog stance.

She always had a slow start and usually missed her first ten houses. Instead of doing the pitch, she'd knock once, wait five seconds, and leave with ass high on shoulder because they didn't open the door. If someone *did* open the door fast enough she'd say, "Here go some Nutty Crunch and some cookies," and stand there tapping her foot, hoping they'd say no so she could tell them what to do with the two dollars they didn't have in the first place. Bad would come running to drag her away, and Weber would have to pack up the crew real fast and hustle us to the next town.

I know. I was forced to work with Shawanda once last summer. If she wasn't getting loud with the customers she was always disappearing into someone's house for hours, and would come out after selling just one box, or sometimes none, and have money missing. Meanwhile, I was blowing High Man, waiting for her to catch up before I could move on to the next block.

Bad was no better.

I also worked with him once last summer. He was forever leaving his route to cop drugs, rap to chicks, get some shade, and BS around because he finally sold a few cans. Couldn't just BS on his own time—had to drag me in on it. "Aw man, let's chill. We done sold five cans."

Bad had my vote for the Laziness Poster Child. Everything was too much effort. His lower lip stayed dry because it took too much muscle to pull it up to meet his top lip. His eyelids stayed half-closed for the same reason. He hunched over, weaving from side to side when he walked, instead of straightening all six-feet-three of him and walking tall. One thing, though. Bad had style to his slackness. When he'd trip over the shoelaces he never tied, he'd recover by making it look like a dance step. The doo rag that he wore to protect waves that no one ever saw was always color-coordinated to match his sweats.

His pitch was about slouching up to a customer's door with his eyes cast down, knowing they wasn't gonna buy and giving them every reason to say no because he was too slow. After skipping most of his houses he'd come to the pick-up point throwing his hands up and crying, "Bad area, man. Bad area. No tale, no sale." Then he and Shawanda would fight on the way back to the office and then all the way to 171st Street and Liberty Avenue in Jamaica.

"Throw two more cans of Crunch in my case," I said to Weber.

"Can you handle it?"

"Light stuff."

"I like your style," Weber said, making room in my case for the extras. "In over your head and talking your way out."

Not to be outdone, Carmello took an extra four boxes of cookies and put them in his case.

Weber left us to scout out new areas, which meant Carmello would accept offers to go inside houses. No one ever asked me if I was thirsty or if I had to go to the bathroom, but women were always throwing these courtesies out to Mello. I'd clock him sometimes. Fifteen, twenty minutes.

I went to my first house, knocked, and got no answer, then moved on to the next house. No one was home. I stopped for a second to check out Carmello. He never smiled when he did his pitch. Didn't care if you bought or closed the door. But when he gave the line about how this job kept him out of trouble, you believed him. Women looked at Carmello and instantly wanted to help the juvenile delinquent walk the line between crime and salvation. Not that any of these housewives thought he was a nice boy for their daughters. But they were good for heavy donations.

"Must have been some glass of water," I called over to him.

"Water's water," he said, maybe ten dollars up on his sales as he went for his third house.

I was up to my third house. Rang bell. Again, no answer. Wasting time. Let's move. My next house showed signs of life. On the TV, a talk show audience was booing a speaker. I rang the bell and prepared to be Dinizulu, foreign exchange student. Harmless yet aggressive. A woman's voice came from behind the door. "Who is it?" The voice belonged to someone who was about fifty, lonely, in need of a snack. She peered through the window. I was right.

"It is Dinizulu, mum."

"I don't need none today, thank you."

"Please, mum. Do not shut de door on a nation. This will only take but a moment of your important time."

The door opened. The chain rested across her nose.

I spoke swiftly, smiled, and aimed for her pupils. "Surely, mum, you have heard de song 'We Are de World.' And is it not true? When de peoples of me homeland are faced with de famine, we are all faced with de famine. Do you not agree, mum?"

"Well, yes, I . . ."

"Then perhaps you wish to donate to the cause directly, mum?"

She undid the chain and opened the door. "Whatcher sellin'?"

"We have Miss Minerva's assortment of cookies, and de World Famous Nutty Crunch. A modest two dollars and fifty cents apiece."

I made the sale, said "Ungawa"—something I once heard on a Tarzan movie—and broke out into a joyous chorus of "We Are the World." Two dollars went into my left pocket, two quarters into my right pocket. Later I would duck into a candy store and exchange the coins from my donations for bills.

I knew I wasn't exactly up to speed, but I did sell a few. Carmello had worked his block and waited for me to finish out the other houses on my side. "D. Whattup?"

"You tell me."

"One block, six boxes. An easy day."

"Pure luck."

"Skill. They wanted pizza." Carmello shook his box as proof of a light day's work. I wasn't worried. I was just warming up, whereas he'd probably max his sales by the third block and would be down for the rest of the day.

We sat on the curb. "So catch me up on what's been going on," I said.

"I'm a daddy." He beamed.

"Again? Tell me something new." Mello already had two kids littered around town.

"Gila's the mommy. I nailed her, man." He was especially

proud of that because Ymangila didn't fall for Mello instantly, wouldn't come to the window when he'd whistle up to her, and made him meet her parents. It figured. Mello wouldn't be happy until he wore her down into complete submission. Now he was probably tired of her.

"Still messing with her?"

He shrugged. "Off and on."

"So what else is new?"

"Remember those two clowns working Dave's crew?" I didn't, but to hurry the story along I nodded. "They made a little money and disappeared in the subway and that was that."

"Deep."

"Bad got ripped off for his gold chain. He gave it up without a fight. Me? I'd die before I let someone punk me. Give up my stuff without a bruise on my body?" His voice got loud. His disgust for Bad was strong. Too strong. "Bad just walked away, happy to be alive. What a punk."

"We can't all be the Man of Steel," I said in Bad's defense, knowing I'd have done the same thing.

"That's true. But we can't all be Einstein either." Then he broke into this broad grin. The kind the girls liked.

"What?"

"You, man. Thought you was going to some college."

"I did. Checked it out. Decided it's not for me, man. Not that I couldn't do it. College is too slow. I'm sitting in a red Porsche, stuck in the granny lane. Everything I said was fast talk on a slow track. Those Ph.D.'s had to rethink their whole program just to keep up with the speed of light."

"So what. You didn't dig that college thing. At least you got that far. Me? I never dug school, which was cool because school didn't dig me too tough neither." He pounded on his cardboard case until the top flap caved in. "I wanted to go when I was little, but my moms waited too late to take me. Too busy dating, I guess." Then he laughed. "Dig. I was eight in the first grade. They kept bouncing me from English to bilingual to Special Ed classes 'cause I wouldn't talk. They said I was the biggest problem ever walked in a classroom. Hey, know how many times I was in third grade? School? I got school in Spofford. Some, Rikers. Now that's school. What they got to teach, you don't want to learn. Me? I take it like a man 'cause it's about survival."

Only Mello could spit up facts like he knocked up his girl, his mother was loose, and that he did God knows what for survival, and make it sound like a cough. I couldn't let him know I was impressed, even though I was.

I got up from the sidewalk and tapped Mello's shoulder. "Listen up. Hear that?"

"Hear what?"

"That. The sound of the speed of light. Whipped by ya pretty fast, didn't it?"

"So what you tryin' to say?"

"Too fast for ya, Man of Steel? Shall I play it back in slow mo?" I got up from the curb and dusted off my pants. "I'm gunning for you, Mello. With this here." I pointed to my head. "I'm taking High Man."

Mello looked at me like he couldn't really take me seriously. But he got up, accepting the challenge, and we were at it again.

THE MAN FROM KRYPTON

IT WAS try-out day at the zoo. With summer ending, the crews had to be replenished with dropouts who could work school hours through fall and winter. So far, the ad that ran yesterday had attracted six sales trainees who stuck out sitting among us vets. They actually believed they could "earn summer dollars plus gain marketing experience."

With myself as an exception, the outer office was filled with social misfits unable to get work elsewhere. For me, sitting on the bench was temporary. A goof. An adventure. Loose change. An alter alias. I could always take off and fly in any direction I pointed. Even Princeton.

I shook up a carton of o.j. and sat next to Mello and Mikie. Shawanda and Bad sat on a bench facing four recruits. Out of the four of them, only the girl who had just been interviewed had sales potential. The two guys sitting next to her were clearly weekers: work one week, hang out till payday, then vanish. The third guy kept looking around the outer office, changing his mind about the whole thing. He wore a light brown suit and had probably brought a resume that would stay folded in his breast pocket.

Two other recruits, a brother and sister, were being tried out by Jack and Weber in the office. The door was open. I could see these two were losers. Their chances of being sales trainees died as soon as they spoke. They couldn't look Jack or Weber in the eye or do the pitch without apologizing and forgetting the product names or their own names. Between the two of them they shared an ounce of heart and the same pitiful face.

I listened for a while, checking out their mannerisms. So polite and scared. Out of state. No. Down South. Her voice was a touch above a whisper. His was all mumble. They were petrified. When the first customer slammed the door in their faces they'd stand there with incredulous expressions just before the tears began to roll. Or they'd tremble at the door, asking, "Won't you please buy some if it's not too much trouble," all the while backing away.

That was not how it worked. Your stance had to be aggressive but friendly. You smiled when you said, "I have change for a twenty . . . Can I put you down for three?" You had plan B handy to deal with those ready-made excuses not to buy. Your case was not a two-ton box, but an opportunity to skim donations above your commission. You pitched them. Threw some style on it, some guilt, and a nice "You'll be helping a very deserving cause"—blink, blink—and you were making money.

Every high seller had a style. Mikie's was the cute thing. Mello was a stone ladies' man. Mine was a success formula: Sales equals skill over confidence. Shawanda and Bad had no style. They also didn't sell, and if they *did* sell, it was always for two bills and no better.

"Try it again. This time let's see that smile," Jack coached patiently, although it was obvious they weren't worth training.

The girl cleared her throat. A fuzzy sound followed. "I-I-I'm Sharon and I-I-I-I with the Summer Action Program and I has s-s-some Miz 'Nerba's sorted cookies an' dey tasis good. Dey's only two dollars and de proceeds go to helping kee-ids l-l-like m-m-me stays employed and out of trouble."

"Better. Better." Jack nodded sincerely.

There was something so sad about these two that it just might work. People might just believe that they were victims of some catastrophe and give them money and tell them to keep the cookies and candy. I gave Mello a tap. "Dig them." Mello was deep into the sports section of the *News* and could care less.

The only prospect worth training was the cute little girl sitting on the bench opposite us. Despite having been interviewed and knowing what the job was about, she was still interested. She appeared to be a young sixteen. Bright looking, but not hungry for the job. Sun-colored skin, nice hair pulled back, petite body, slender legs, casually dressed in a denim skirt, loose shirt, flat shoes—no doubt designer's—on her tiny feet. She was ladylike. An odd quality for a girl in the crews.

Mello and I would have been there first, but seeing that Bad was already talking to her we just lay back to check out his rap.

"Oooh, hello miss lady. Can I know your name?"

She looked up at him and was simple enough to show him some teeth. "I'm Karen. And who are you?"

"My name is Robert. 'Round the way, they call me Honey Love. Here, they call me Bad, short for Bad Area Bob. Know why? 'Cause when it comes to selling there is none badder! Are you following, sweetheart?"

Bad was a funny dude to sit down and check out. He was a comic, rapping his heart out, going into poetic gestures to accompany every little pause like he was a background singer, with expressions and dance steps synchronized. He thought he was being articulate when he really sounded like a clown saying "I is Bozo" with his best foot forward.

He turned up the volume for us, his audience.

It was too soon to laugh because the girl was going for it. Maybe because Bad was someone to talk to in a new place, or she was that cute kind of girl who was used to being rapped to, or because Bad was a veteran. She uncrossed her legs, flashed another smile, and said in a lazy voice trying to sound a little older, "I like that Honey Love sounding name."

The only question was how long Shawanda would let this go on. Bad had to be stupid to miss the steam rising and spraying from Shawanda's head.

True, the new girl was fine. In that regard, there was no contest between her and Shawanda. Not that Shawanda wasn't nice looking. She could have been. Well, maybe. She was just too dangerous, often boasting of how she dealt with her six brothers. The cry of "fight fight" and "your girls 'gainst mine" was going to follow her for life. A guy would have to be crazy for rapping to her because Shawanda liked flexing her muscles too much to yield.

Although she and Bad were far from officially talking, she considered him property. Not that Bad knew it. Nor did he know that you didn't disrespect Shawanda to her face. Shawanda never backed down from an opportunity to demonstrate what she could do when provoked.

As though he couldn't see the warning signs, Bad stuck his head in the office door where Jack was interviewing and said, "Here go my new partner, Miss Karen." He sat closer to Karen, telling her how he would look out for her, show her how to sell big, and how they would be a winning team.

Uh oh! World Famous Nutty Crunch winding up and coming in at twelve o'clock. You knew she was going to do it. Warn him? No, Mello said. Sit back and dig the cartoons.

Bonk! Right off of Bad's head.

"Whatchoo do that for?"

Shawanda ignored her wounded partner and went straight for the girl. "Who you think you are? Pushing me around like I'm invisible." Shawanda was in the girl's face, daring her to do something about it. The girl was stunned. Shawanda got louder. "How you gonna come in here talking to him—you don't even know what the story is!"

"Hey, look—" the girl surrendered with both hands up, letting you know she had seen her share of scrapes.

"No, girlfriend. You look. That's *my* partner until I say so."

Bad jumped up. "Well I'm saying—"

"You, shut the hell up. I'm talking here." Shawanda pushed Bad aside with one hand. "This is new ground! Learn the rules," she declared. "You wanna live right? Act right." Shawanda didn't sit down until she made Karen "yes" her like she was Shawanda's child. Bad, being the Class A punk that he was, squatted next to Shawanda and left Karen hanging. Karen tried to recoup her losses with a blasé front when she felt everyone staring. Then Weber came out and said, "Karen, you're with Dave's crew," settling it once and for all. They sent the brother and sister act out to practice and motioned one of the recruits to come in. The brother and sister sat on the far edge of Shawanda's bench, hoping she wouldn't notice them.

"So what's the Jets talking about?" I tried to talk to Carmello as he read the paper.

"Ain't nothing." Mello didn't look up. "I don't even know why I bother reading this. They lost again."

"Well, it's only exhibition games," I said. "But can you dig where this guy's coming from? I don't see it."

Mello grunted. His eyes roamed the story about free agents, which was placed directly below a photo from last night's game. The photo was of the intercepted quarterback's face at the moment of agony. "See story on page 56" was at the lower left edge of the photo in fine print. Still, Mello made like he was reading about last night's game from that article.

"Says here he was intercepted three times in the third quarter. It was all downhill from there."

"The offensive line is the real problem," I played along.

Mello peered down into the paper, and pulled from the free agents story that "they need to be traded. Too old to cut it." He then rolled up the paper in a hard tube and twisted it. "Want this?"

"Naw, man," I said, not sure how he meant that.

He unrolled the paper and let his eyes wander.

I should have busted him. The big jock. Mello couldn't read a word. He was looking at the pictures, pretending to follow an article.

Now it all made sense. Like Mello always asking how many blocks to the pick-up point instead of reading the street signs. And how he always walked boldly inside yards with "NO SOLICITORS" or "ATTACK DOG ON DUTY" posted on fences. It also explained why he used to talk about getting a driver's license like it was the unattainable dream. He wanted to go for construction. Drive a tractor or operate a forklift. Said the DMV wouldn't give him a license because he was an ex-offender. Naw, man. He couldn't get past the eye chart. He probably went to the DMV, was given ten different forms, then said to hell with it.

Big guy, stumbling around in the dark. Technically blind, depending on others to relay the world to him. It wasn't even that bilingual thing. He couldn't read Spanish, and he couldn't read English. All the time he was passing me Ymangila's letters I thought he was bragging. Naw. The blind man needed a reading-eye dawg.

Flash:

"Want a laugh?" he said, holding up a peach envelope. "Check this out. Go ahead. Read it. Have you dyin'."

I was curious since I had never had a serious letter from a girl. Why not. I read Ymangila's letter.

"I can barely make it out," Mello said. "You know how females write. All squiggly and fancy. Can't get a Q from a U," he joked.

"Sounds hot to me," I said. With five years of Spanish and having been introduced to the vernacular, I got the gist of Ymangila's letter. At the time I didn't understand Mello's trouble with her handwriting because her penmanship was impeccable.

"Hot? What . . . that? Which part? Read it. Probably no big thrill." Mello laughed it off like he was used to getting these letters. Knowing Mello, it was word.

"No big thrill," I said. "She's only talking about your nine inches of love."

"Gimme that." Mello snatched his letter back. "She knows it's ten." He crumpled the peach stationery into a hard little ball and threw it far. "Why they do that? Write this stupid stuff when they can say it to your face? Just for that I won't write her back. I'll leave her hanging. Then she'll have to call me."

Back:
You big, illiterate dummy. You couldn't write her if you wanted to. You couldn't read her a get-well card over the

phone. I'll bet you wouldn't know your own name if you saw it in print.

I watched him pretending to read the paper. Sure, there was some left to right eye movement, but the rhythm was jerky like his eyes were running scared. I wondered what he saw in place of ". . . this year in arbitration." Did the letters jump around and tease him? Did the words look Czechoslovakian? Maybe he knew numbers. Could make out the stats. But how would he know what teams or players they belonged to?

This was too good to be true. I could be the man from Krypton. Blow his whole Superman thing. Hold up a newspaper to his red and blue cape. Hey Superman, read this! I could laugh at him. Laugh in his face for no apparent reason, at any time of day, and let him think about it. Think about it. *Can you do that, Superman?*

This was killing me. Here I was, sitting this close to Superman, with a big bag of Kryptonite up my sleeve, knowing I could be the one to squash Mello in public.

The only thing that was saving Mello was the code, and the fact that he never threw his 195 pounds up against my 125, so what would I look like crushing Mello for no reason?

My guess was Mello didn't know there was a code. Even if I explained that we had this unwritten law that protected both his kingdom and mine, would he get it? Hell no. The knights and the fellowship of the roundtable were in a book beyond his reach.

But I'd get my chance. One day he'd make a move on me, the crowd would be waiting for my comeback, and I'd have my arsenal.

All the same, I hated wasting a good laugh. He did amuse me, sitting there looking tough and stupid, pretending to read the paper. I gave him credit, though. The paper was right side up. It wasn't turned to world events or the business section like he would care. And unlike the average dummy who broadcasts his ignorance, Mello kept his to himself.

Mello, you're an all right dude. But I'm gunnin' for ya, guy. I'm gonna shoot you down one day when you're standing tall like Superman. I'll pull out my Kryptonite and crush you like a dry leaf. And the cool thing will be you'll dig it. Nothing personal, just about knighthood.

It was time to head out and sell. Karen went with Dave's crew. The brother and sister were given the option to go with Dave or stay and practice. They stayed. The guy in the light brown suit was supposed to ride with us. Instead of going to the van, he went in the opposite direction and didn't look back. We got stuck with Wingo and Dwayne, the two guys who had "weeker" written all over them. As long as Weber didn't split up Mello and me, I didn't care if the weekers sold or not. Mello, Mikie, and I could really pick up the slack for the crew. With just the three of us, we could still beat Dave's full crew.

Weber dropped us off on Rutledge Avenue in the Williamsburg section of Brooklyn. "Don't let these first two blocks stop you," he said, driving away. "It picks up."

It didn't take a genius to know that we had been deserted in a no-sale area that didn't want our loud intrusion. This wasn't just another block but another world, and we were seven outlaws trying to walk among Hasidic Jews. The women who peered through windows either pulled down their shades or shooed us away as we approached their walkways. "It's only goddamn candy!" Mello yelled in frustration at women who wouldn't look at his face. He gave up and started walking past his houses. No doubt Bad, Shawanda, and the weekers were doing the same thing, though I wouldn't have been surprised if Mikie was pushing his pixie nose up against screens while doing monkey tricks for kids who might cajole their parents into buying.

Since I had already established who was who on a scale of superiority, I felt obliged to lift Mello's spirits and get things rolling. This called for one of the side bets we had devised to make us sell harder and make the day spin faster. I watched Mello walking past his houses. He didn't seem like the Man of Steel. He seemed like an ant. An illiterate ant. I called over, "What's the game plan? A little free style? Fair game? Or how about High Man draw?"

"High Man's okay with me," Mello said.

"All right. High Man draw it is," I said. "Pick-up point's in what, eight blocks? Loser pays High Man fifty cents on a sale."

"Okay."

"No hustles. No donations. Just straight skill," I added. Mello said, "So," like he could handle it. Of course he'd cheat. Get nervous toward his last block, spot some woman he could hustle for a heavy donation, and get rid of the boxes so it would look like he sold them. I wasn't worried. Mello was going to need all the help he could get.

I felt unstoppable. I rang every doorbell while Mello continued to walk past his houses. Once I accepted that Hasidic Jews would not, could not, be sold to, I relaxed and made a game of it. If I made one sale, just one, then it would prove that I had the skill. As I stood there, crystallizing the plan, an old man peeked my mind and bought a can of Nutty Crunch. I picked up steam. Two houses down, I found that not only was I skilled, but I was gifted, which was just the high I needed crossing the avenue to work a new area.

Everything from that point on was just too easy. It didn't matter how many times the complexion of the neighborhood changed within the next couple of blocks. For every block I had a face, a voice, a manner. In no time, I sold out my first case to Germans, Poles, and Italians.

My case was now empty. The last thing I wanted was to get cold waiting around when I could be selling. Luck always rolls with momentum. I had to keep selling. I motioned for Mello to throw me something to sell. His motion back indicated that I could forget it.

Finally Weber arrived to restock our cases. Mello insisted on taking an extra piece to sell. He said it was so there wouldn't be any ties and any question as to who was High Man. I looked in his case and saw that he had six unsold pieces. "When we ante up, just make mine dollars," I said, and moved on to the young urban professionals who occupied the condos overlooking the bridge. They were particularly easy to sell to. Make them feel old and out of it and they were all too eager to buy. I couldn't let the opportunity go to waste. I started taking donations and jacking up the price to three dollars so I could make a killing in addition to what I would win off of Mello. I racked up in a clean sweep, selling two-thirds of my second case in the condos.

"Three more blocks," I called over to Mello, who was gaining on me. I wasn't worried. I had the Kryptonite. Besides, it was no fun winning High Man draw without any true sport.

It would be five soon. I looked ahead to where our sales territory hit a dead end before the highway. I shifted into low gear to sell to Blacks, close out the day, and collect on High Man draw. My winnings would make a nice down payment on a silk and linen blazer that only came in one size—mine. With two cans and two boxes in my case, the real issue was choice: who would be lucky enough to get them.

I surveyed my last block of brownstones. They looked good. My only regret was not canvassing this area first. With a block like this I could carry a forty-can load on an ice cream day and still be up. The ceramic knickknacks on the windowsills gave them away. These people bought any old thing. They looked that easy.

I plotted my sweep. First hit the two women unloading grocery bags from their van. They should be ready to buy. They bought half the store anyway, so what's another three bills? Next would be the basement apartment where music was coming from and the women were pointing to, showing their disapproval. Had to be a party going on in the basement. For my last sale I marked a young woman sitting out on a porch with her three kids. I assumed that there was no man in the family and rehearsed my "I'm gonna make it all right for two dollars" pitch. Her children jubilantly played tag, the youngest was "it." The woman could be twenty-two and her kids about three, four, and five. Her head was hung. She didn't notice me yet, but she would. I'd talk to her. Probably didn't get much conversation being tied down like that. It'd make her feel good. She'd be grateful. Pull out the purse. Depending on how good her conversation was, I might even give her the last box and square it out of my donations. A kind of goodwill thing.

I descended upon my next two sales. "Good evening, ladies, and please pardon my interruption," I said, using the manners to appeal to their age. "Now how can I interest you in this fine box of cookies when you've already bought out an entire supermarket?" I held up a box of Miss Minerva's Assorted Cookies, glancing to see who between them would be the mark. "They're delicious, nonfattening—if you only eat two—and it's for a worthy cause."

The little one's eyes brightened. She smiled weakly. The big one pressed her lips sternly. I could see I was up against Good Cop–Bad Cop.

"How much are they?" asked Good Cop, hoping Bad Cop would bail her out.

"Only thirty dollars."

"Thirty dollars! You can keep it," Bad Cop jumped in, glad to show off how tough she was.

"You got me," I admitted. "Seriously, they're only three dollars apiece, and your contribution will benefit our youth employment program." I could never give the line about keeping kids such as myself out of trouble. I looked too clean. Destined for success.

"Yeah, well, I knew it wasn't no thirty dollars," Bad Cop said, digging into her purse.

I took their six dollars, put four in my left pocket, and two in my right. Unbelievable! They had bought twenty bags of groceries—at least three of those bags were filled with desserts—and what did these two women do? Paid six dollars for ninety-nine cents worth of cookies. This should make a good story for the ride back.

I rewound my pitch and went down the steps leading to the basement apartment, knowing a few things about my victim before seeing her face. The potted plants in the window said she. The smell emanating from the cracked window said reeferhead. From the music (a woman dragging the blues), it was clear that she saw herself as being sophisticated, with big ideas about world situations, and was creative in some way. Probably looked down on industrious types such as myself, because why else would she be home at 5:00 smoking dope? And, unless I missed my guess, she wore her hair some "natural" way to let you know where she was coming from. No sooner had I put my finger on the buzzer, the screen door flew open. A skinny woman with sharp facial features, a long neck, and hair like she had been wrestling stood in the doorway. She cut off my first word by putting her hand up like a traffic cop signaling me not to even try it.

"Baby, you want some of this mess?" she called back to the other room. Another voice responded.

"Some of this candy an' shit, that's what," she yelled back louder. "Gimme a dollar."

"It's two," I corrected.

"Damn. Baby, go in my bag and get me two dollars."

The bird neck woman came down on me with her reefer breath.

"You so daggone slow. Cain'tcha see this boy *needs* this two dollars?" Her laughter cut across the boundary between us, whipping my face like she had forgotten I was there. She gave me the money, dug into my case without my permission, and shook the two cans of Crunch, choosing the one that she thought was heavier. When she slammed the door I could feel the film of her laughter sticking to my skin.

I knew I must have stood there longer than I should have, trying to figure out what had just happened. I walked away from the basement apartment and passed the woman with her children. The little one was still "it," running in circles.

Mello was leaning against a car, drinking a soda. His case was flattened, and was sticking up in the deli's garbage can. Mello was a cool and righteous knight. We both knew that he'd won the draw and that I had to pay up, but he wouldn't mention it. He'd just take the money and say something off the mark like only Mello could.

I crossed over, hearing the sound of my last can roll from one end of the narrow case to the other. I didn't want to smile or look like it mattered. Instead, I searched for something to focus on, pretending to read a sign.

EIGHTH ROW, CENTER PEW

"DID anybody call yesterday?"

"No. Debra Jordan didn't call, if that's what you want to know."

"Not her."

"Jonelle didn't call."

"Not her either—you know so much."

"Tanya didn't call."

"Look Kerri, did I get a call from Wendy?"

"No ... I don't think so." She paused, squinted thoughtfully, then shook her head. "Nope, nope, nope. She didn't call for sure."

"Are you sure?"

"What did I say?"

I took my spoon and flicked a cornflake at her. "Remember, you're speaking to your elder."

"Dinizulu, you make me laugh. Hah, hah, hah."

"You're a raghead. You know that?"

"But my friends still call."

"What's that supposed to mean?"

"She thinks you're sewer sweat. No," Kerri retracted. "She thinks you're the stuff that looks up to sewer sweat." She shot an accusing glance. "Can you blame her?"

"Did she call? Where did you hear that?"

"From your face."

"Little sister, you know nothing," I answered, although she wasn't entirely off base. It had been almost a week since I had seen Wendy. I expected her to at least call before she went to school. Apologize. Make a joke. But if that's the way she wanted to leave things, then fine. Leave it.

Kerri grinned at me from across the table, pretending to know something. I looked past her face to get the correct time from the wall clock. I adjusted my watch. Kerri was still grinning. I pointed at the clock. "Eat up."

Lydia was just about ready to leave. Lydia lived for Sundays. It was in her walk. Her heels tapped Morse code on the linoleum. *It is Sunday. It is D-Day. Dress, eat, and pray. Dress, eat, and pray.*

Her perfume entered the kitchen. "Is everyone ready?" she practically sang, while inspecting our attire. She smoothed back Kerri's hair and gave me a quick once-over. "You really should wear a tie," habit forced her to say when it was obvious that a tie would kill my collar. I ignored her. *I'm going, aren't I? Don't push it.*

Lydia never forced us to attend Sunday services, but she didn't mean for us to refuse the invitation either. She always zeroed in on you while you were hemming and hawing, trying to solidify the excuse that sounded right the night before. Be slow enough and you found yourself sitting in Allen African

Methodist Episcopal Sunday morning, staring mindlessly at the backs of folks' heads. Eighth row, center pew.

Vernon was exempt. It was understood that Vernon, in his pajamas and slippers, still reading the paper, had a standing invitation to escort his family to services. This was an implied invitation that was never vocalized in front of Kerri and me, but one that was repeatedly opened and closed between Lydia and Vernon.

Vernon Watson did not go in for the conventions of Christianity or any other religions that mirrored European worship. When I was ten he told me how Christianity marked the beginning of imperialism in Africa. "First they sent the missionaries, then they sent the cannons." (All this because I had asked him to come to services and hear me recite the Scripture of the Week.)

In those days I enjoyed tripping Dad up in his principles. It was like a game, and my prize was the stupid look on his face when his tongue didn't quite know where to go. This was easy to accomplish, being that Vernon felt it necessary to entertain the inquisitive mind.

"So why'd you marry her?" I had asked when Dad was putting down Lydia's devotion to Christianity. *Her,* the daughter of an African Methodist Episcopal reverend. *Her,* a walking monument to the Perfect Negro in America, everything Dad hated. *Her,* the woman who never missed an opportunity to serve on some church committee. *Her,* with hat, gloves, stole, and stones just so on a Sunday. And although we lived across the park from the church, *her* never failed to have the Lincoln washed and polished Saturday, only to drive two blocks and a left turn to Allen A.M.E. on Sunday.

"Because I loved her," was Vernon's simple answer. "And always will."

I don't know what illed me most—Vernon's expression of

love or knowing that he loved her more than those principles he quit jobs and went to jail for. Love or no, Dad never set foot inside Allen A.M.E. on Sunday, and it was safe to say he never would. For Lydia's sake, however, he'd offer a nice word or two about the community services sponsored by the church, saying, "At least they serve the people."

As soon as we could read, Vernon assigned both Kerri and me books on the philosophies and religions of the world with Lydia's hesitant permission. The understanding was that we would make our own decision about religion.

Somehow Lydia's smileless "Coming to services?" firmly pushed aside Islam, Hinduism, Shintoism, or any other religions. Truthfully, no matter how much we read, Christmas loot always sounded better than some intangible reward like oneness or spiritual peace. Besides, when I was a kid my calendar was based on the two things that most of these world religions did not recognize: Christmas and birthdays. Then, too, Dad had not formally joined anything, which gave Lydia a stronghold on our religious training. This made Nana Dee happy. Nana worshiped at Calvary Baptist on the other side of town, and always wanted to have us christened in her church. Knowing what Dad had planned for us, she gladly settled upon us being raised as Christians any way we could get it.

Lydia put the keys in my hand and gave me that beam of pride that was supposed to mean "You're finally a man. Here's the car." I didn't get excited. My license was getting colder by the minute, just sitting in my wallet for ID purposes. Lydia stood there smiling, waiting for me to say, "Gee, Mom. Thank you for trusting me with this honor," like I didn't know I was only driving two blocks, a light, and a left turn. Park. Open her door, lock up, and give her back the keys.

I put the keys in my pocket and finished my milk.

As we left I called, "All right Dad."

Vernon just nodded and said, "Son."

Kerri had not grown out of planting a wet smack on Daddy's forehead, then giggling all embarrassed, like she done did something. She ran to the car making that kindergarten *clang, clang* with those patent leather shoes, unaware that her breasts jumped underneath her dress when she ran like that.

"Horses gallop. Young ladies glide," Lydia said, instead of buying her a bra or telling her to step back and dig herself.

Kerri was in her own world with no windows and no doors. If she had half a clue that she was being watched, she wouldn't act so goofy. She was in no hurry to turn thirteen, although she did insist that the number of braided antennae on her round little head be reduced to one ponytail.

I took a good look at her. Kerri was a goofy puppy. She either looked happy, silly, or deep, as in book deep. She didn't sport the look yet. The one that they all wore by the age of thirteen or fourteen. *I got the thing, now suffer, you dawg.* Kerri didn't know about or care about the look, let alone notice boys. She was in a deep sleep. The guy who was going to shake her would have to go through COBOL, BASIC, dolls, and a lot of silliness just to say hello.

I wish I could talk to you, little sis, I thought. Just look at you. Destined to get Lydia's face. A stone killer. Don't even know how to play it off, do you? Just as honest as honest is stupid. Grinning broadly for all the world to see your teeth.

I opened the front door of the Lincoln for Lydia, the back for Kerri. Lydia settled in like she was being chauffeured to the airport. For two minutes' worth of drive she was a statuette and played it to no end. Didn't make a move until I opened her door and offered my arm. Mom was too cool and loved it. If I did get married, my wife would have to be a queen and know it.

We arrived in time to blend in with the "first families" of

Allen, who were all marching up the concrete steps. The Callendars. "First" black family to successfully move into Rosedale without being bombed out, row six, left pew. The Duncans. First family to hold membership at some country club out on the Island, row five, center pew. The Abel-Beys. First family to donate a wing to a foundling home, row four, center pew. And so on. We were a first family of some sort, though I wasn't quite sure of what.

We socialized. I almost enjoyed being Lydia's escort although the enjoyment didn't last long. She introduced me to people whom I'd known all my life like I was a visiting relative. Gag me with a stick. She didn't let up: "You know my son who's graduated at the top of his class and is going to Princeton this fall . . ." My name was never mentioned. I excused myself to stand with members of the teen club, who were no doubt discussing the upcoming bus ride.

Standing around with them and their silliness was no better than dealing with Lydia and hers. They were only a year or two behind me, but they seemed so young. Their irrelevant talk would carry them for weeks. For the moment they were caught up in "who likes whom." They were trying to push together the club secretary, who pretended to be mousy but was the engineer of the whole thing, and her victim, a tenor in the choir who allowed himself to be pawned.

Their game was so obvious. I just stood back and dug it, thinking how only a few weeks ago I was the center of the gossip whirlwind that kept them on edge. The act of thinking about it was grounds enough to tear up my teen club card. I didn't belong with them either. I turned to walk away.

"My dear Mr. Watson. You missed the last six meetings and you know we're having an outing. How do you expect to ride with us if you don't sign up? Luckily we saved you a spot. That's right. You owe me fifteen bucks, so pay up quick 'cause

I'm not Rockefeller. Well? Don't just stand there trying to be too, too sophisticated. Where've you been all this time?"

I didn't have to turn around to identify the rapid chatter and sarcasm. It belonged to Evelyn "The Mouth" Moses, who was asking on behalf of Jonelle Spenser, her mostly mute cousin.

"College orientation. Just got back," I answered.

Jonelle looked up, giving me the soulful "is it too late?" flash of eyelash. I stared her down and thought, Yes, dear. Much too late.

"Sittin' with us? Might as well. Won't see you till Christmas, and we just might forget your face," Evelyn said, maneuvering for Jonelle.

"I promised Moms I'd sit with her," I said, using the right amount of regret so Jonelle didn't come off looking like a fool. I got out of the bus ride and promised to pay Evelyn back the fifteen dollars next week. Feeling charitable, I added that I'd stop by and visit before I left for Princeton.

Then I stopped. It dawned on me. I wasn't going. I had to tell everyone that I wasn't going.

I choked. I didn't want anyone to see IT in my face. Especially Evelyn "The Mouth" Moses, who would major in communications one day, go on to anchor the six o'clock news, and be heard all through America.

I left them to find Lydia and Kerri. Evelyn and Jonelle would evaluate how it went, while I already knew. As fine as Jonelle was, she was a minister's daughter, which would thrill Lydia to no end. Lydia would love to roast, boil, and bake in Jonelle Spenser's honor, and nothing would make her happier than to give me little talks about "how we treat church daughters, no matter how big and brown her legs are." The other strike against Jonelle was being close kin to Evelyn, who didn't know when to shut up or when to disappear. I mean, if I made a move on Jonelle, Evelyn would feel it first.

I took my mother's arm. Kerri followed. *Clang, clang.*

The procession began with the entrance of the choirs. The male chorus. The Voices of Victory. The Cherub Choir. The ministers were in place at the pulpit. Kerri and Lydia had turned to Matthew to follow the Scripture of the Week. I made a weak effort to stay with it, but I really wanted to drift. Phrases were planted in my ear. "My Father has given me all things. No one knows the Son except the Father . . ." was the last thing I heard clearly. I drifted further, but the reader was like a drum beating "My Father, My Father" with a force and rhythm that made the words impossible to lose. My body was still. My gaze was toward the pulpit; my mind took another turn. "My Father" was on the outside, trying to get in. I shook it off.

There is a sheet of paper with writing. It is an essay. My best work. A red D sits high in the right-hand corner. Red comments fill the margins. "Grammar and syntax show mastery of basic skills; paper says nothing." The word excess *sprouts several pointing arrows from the left margin. Logic sits next to the main paragraph. This is the paragraph with my persuasive argument. Next to* logic *are double question marks like the ones used to indicate a grand chess error.*

Blink Princeton away.

I snapped out of it during the liturgy, with my eyes on Mr. Randall's bald spot. I noticed Morris sitting next to old man Randall, and I figured he was as absent as I was.

Morris Randall and I never talked or hung out, mainly because of the six years between us and the fact that he was always away at school, which also included years of military academy. But now that I thought about it, Morris and I should have had a lot in common. We were both firstborn sons. We were both expected to do no less than excellent.

I could feel him out. We just might click. I could tell him

what was really going on. Ask him if he ever felt like he wasn't Ivy League material, and if it was possible to bounce back from zero. If Morris said that I could do it, then I would go back to Princeton in the fall and give it a shot. If anyone knew about IT, the Ivy League Terror, Morris did. Morris was proof. The actual proof. And he was right there. Row five, right pew.

I came in on the hymn louder than usual. Lydia turned and looked at me in amazement. I kept on singing. My resolve was firm. I would get Morris away from old man Randall and confess. I'd even endure a little "Say, little brother" just to admit to someone who just might understand I failed.

I failed.

It wasn't so bad saying it to myself. I failed. I tried breezing through the summer program, and I failed. Then I gave it everything just to see if I could do it, and I failed. No ten ways around it. I failed.

The Voices of Victory were singing and I was feeling okay. Letting loose was what I needed. I felt lighter than a get high. I could take off and fly.

The service had moved past the Invocation, the Free Will Offering, and the Right Hand of Fellowship. *My Father* stayed with me while everything else blended into a mumbo jumbo of familiar steps. The Announcements. Tithes and Offerings. The Gospel. It wouldn't be long. In another hour we'd be joining hands to sing "It'll Be All Right." The recession would follow, and I'd grab Morris in the aisle.

I was rocking side to side waiting for the services to end. I must have looked retarded. I even found myself saying aloud, "My Father, My Father." Lydia thought I was praying and squeezed my hand.

Community announcements. I glanced at my watch. The reverend yielded the pulpit to Mrs. Farley, chair of the education committee, who then asked all of the June graduates to stand. "Stand before God and your community. Stand."

I had no intention of standing. Last year I would have leaped out of my seat, knowing the praises that were to follow. Lydia cleared her throat, but I stayed seated. Then Lydia gave me a swift one in the ankle and I was on my feet. Kerri was already standing along with scads of kindergarten graduates, sixth graders, and other promotees.

The congregation applauded.

I knew this ritual all too well. I used to actually look forward to it. See how long I would remain standing, while everyone else was eliminated. Now I just wanted to disappear.

"Will those who've graduated with honors remain standing."

I couldn't lift my head. This was stupid. Why did they put us through this? And Lydia was sitting there with her neck stretched to the ceiling, eating it up.

"Will those who've graduated in the top five percent of your class remain standing."

I looked up briefly. Morris, Kerri, a few others, and I stood.

"Will those who've graduated class valedictorian remain standing."

Morris and everyone else were seated. Kerri and I were the only ones standing. Kerri's face was radiant and eager. I could hear her giggling. We were told to come to the altar, but I wouldn't move. Kerri tugged at my cuff. I just stood there. Another sharp tap from Lydia's shoe and I was hobbling. Kerri couldn't get up the aisle fast enough, while I trailed reluctantly. Even on soft carpet, Kerri's shoes made that *clang, clang*.

This was a nightmare. The altar was at the end of a long and narrow aisle. Everyone's faces seemed magnified. The reverend was standing there waiting for Kerri and me. Mrs. Farley wanted us to stand before God and our community and tell that lie. Evelyn said something to me, but I didn't hear her. Jonelle's face seemed huge and grotesque. I couldn't look at her. Morris gave me a nonchalant nod like he expected no less from me. Any minute his Jiminy Cricket—looking father would reach out, grab me, and shout, "Let yo' conscience be yo' guide, son!" Kerri was already there, motioning me to speed it up. I was going to be sick.

The congregation's applause sounded and felt like gunfire. We were each presented with a gold plaque and a cash scholarship award. The reverend told the young folks that Kerri and I were models to aspire to. He called us the new leaders. Allen's shining stars. He shoved a microphone under my chin and said, "Tell them, son. Tell them where you'll be in September."

"Dead and buried" was not the answer that he wanted. I said what I was supposed to say. "Princeton."

He took the microphone back. "Did you hear that? Is this not evidence of what you young people can do when you use what He has given you? Is this not evidence?"

The congregation signified that this was evidence. I followed Kerri back to our seats, eighth row, center pew. Lydia was grabbing up the credit in her smile. She took our plaques and envelopes.

I sank down in the pew, putting my head in my hands. Lydia again thought I was praying, and patted my back. The Cherub Choir led us in the sermonic hymn. The reverend was now ready to deliver the sermon, a special message to the young folks. It didn't matter how soon the services ended. It was all over for me. I had been identified in front of nearly a thousand people in Queens as being nearly perfect. Even Morris saluted me, which killed everything.

There was to be no quick getaway after this. A reception

followed. Pictures taken for the church archives. I accepted Jonelle's father's invitation to dinner. I quoted my 98.8 average for the church bulletin. Parents offered to pay me any price to tutor their children and, in short, be a positive influence. Mrs. Farley thought it would be a good idea for me to tutor high school juniors for an SAT group she was setting up for next year. I was also asked to write an inspirational article on the value of education. Lydia accepted these offers, then I went behind her, refusing them.

When Morris and Randall finally made it over to us there was no room to talk. I was cautious about my moves. What if IT was on my face? I just let Randall do the talking, like always, and Morris stood at attention, in agreement with his old man.

Evelyn had all but thrown Jonelle at me. I didn't want to embarrass the girl, so I talked to her, which was no easy thing. Jonelle was in love with me and was too self-conscious to say anything that made sense. The more we talked, the more I regretted accepting her father's dinner invitation. I remembered other plans and apologized.

"I knew the young man was smart," her father said, breaking into the conversation. "Went and found himself the prettiest girl in the entire church."

If Jonelle could have disappeared, she would have. Her father was oblivious to the major embarrassment he had caused. He put his large hand on my shoulder and led me away from his daughter to where the trustees were gathered. There I was, in the center of these old men as they discussed my future. They had it all mapped out. Now that I was too old for the teen club I had to think about my place within the church's organization. As for school, had I declared an academic major yet? Steer clear of those useless subjects—

investment banking is the way to go. Look us up when you get that degree.

Lydia beamed. I was asphyxiated. No one said catch your breath. No one said step back. Be a son. They had their hands on my back. Patting. Pushing. Knowing.

The funny thing about it was that, soon enough, they would know. The shock would have jaws jerking from row one to row forty, and they'd all be scratching their bald heads, trying to retrace the evidence leading up to the big discovery: Denzel Watson is a fake and a failure.

Lydia couldn't understand why I didn't want to drive her back. She let go of my hand fast enough when she saw in my face that I had had it. Lydia wouldn't risk a scene in front of all of these people.

I had to get out of there. I made it through the crowd and stepped out into one of the hottest days of the year. I walked fast and then broke into a run. I had to get home fast. Change my clothes. Sneak out the back before Lydia got home.

I slid my key into the side door and turned the knob like a thief, gripping the knob hard enough so it wouldn't make a sound. I was in. Took off my shoes. Sneaked across the kitchen linoleum. Tiptoed up . . .

I gave up. There he was, sitting in front of the TV watching an exhibition game. He didn't turn around, but he put his lips together to say "umhmm," acknowledging that I was there.

"Collar choking you, son?" There was amusement in his voice like he was in church with us, saw it all, and couldn't help himself. *Son looks like he's down. Let's kick him. This looks like a good spot.*

He knew I was dismissing him, but he wouldn't let it go.

"If you don't want to be bothered don't go," he said. "Don't get an attitude with me."

"She wants us to go," I finally answered.

"You see me jumping up every Sunday? She still love me." Now he sounded like he was getting ready to laugh. I didn't need this.

"That's you, Dad."

"Like hell that's me. That's a man, period." He turned off the TV by remote. His voice changed. "A man thinks things out. Does what his mind tells him to do. Not what everyone wants him to do 'cause it looks right. Son, a man . . ."

I unbuttoned my shirt and thought about pulling something from my closet to wear for my getaway. There was no Sunday crew, but I had to get on a train—anything fast-moving. Dad was set to jaw for another twenty minutes. That was okay, too. I'd find my "staring spot" on the rug until he was done.

HANGMAN

*I*F I WERE a superstitious guy, my teeth would be
rattling. I'd keep a rabbit's foot in my pocket.
I'd leap over sidewalk cracks or count up signs that Wendy's
prediction had come true and that my luck had deserted
me. Yes, things were on the decline. But that still didn't
give Wendy special vision or me a reason to lose touch with
reality.

What I needed was a change, starting with my pitch.
Straighten out one area of my life and everything else would
fall into place. Ditch the refugee from Zululand. Bury the
standard pitch, too. Come up with an approach that would
go with my image, like "For every sale, my college will contribute matching funds for my tuition." I practiced it for
smoothness and ran it by Mello, but he wasn't listening.
Wildness had his mind. Mello was sitting on a bench, rocking

himself back and forth, so that his head kept banging the wall directly behind him.

Weber listened and agreed that I would sell better with this angle. He equated it with major league pitching. You start out with a lot of power. Throw some pretty unbelievable stuff, striking them out one, two, three. Then the pitch gets a little worn. It loses its spin. Before you know it the doors are closing while you're lost in the windup. That's when it's time to try something new.

Okay.

I sold to my first at bat. It was a clean pitch; she went for it. Dug into the apron. Pulled out a Lincoln and gave the high sign for one box, one can. It was a ground-rule double. I felt good. Ready. I approached my next house. Nobody home. Moved on to house three, where a big hand in the window waved me away. Then I lost my next six houses. I crossed over to a new block. I got a guy who wanted to conversate when all I wanted to do was give him a pitch, take his two dollars, and go. He was a geezer with leathery skin, freckles, and a buzz cut—not because it was the style but because he left it that way fifty years back. He had a tugboat tattoo, big yaller dentures, and was bent on giving me advice like he was my equal.

"State schools are just as good as private," he said with teeth sliding side to side in his gums. "Not as expensive, either."

Was this guy serious? Did he know who he had on his front porch? He wasn't talking to Bad, Shawanda, Mello, or Mikie. This was me. Denzel Watson. Addesleigh Park. Italian loafers, dress pants, and one hundred percent cotton polo shirt. He missed the point.

I blew that sale and halfheartedly wound up for the next house. It wasn't totally my fault. No one wanted to do Kew Gardens. Weber should have known that when he made up his crew. It didn't matter how spread out the borough was. Kids from Queens couldn't sell too close to home, and we were all from various parts of Queens: Addesleigh Park, South Jamaica, Jackson Heights, Springfield Gardens. Too much chance of running into someone you know. There you are carrying your case, and you run into your boys. You think fast. Cover with, "I ripped it off a truck," so you don't look like you do this for a living.

As if that weren't enough, you had to watch your back for all the teachers in the area. What teacher didn't live in Kew Gardens? It was an exit or two off the Grand Central, yet far enough to steer clear of those little Black faces from hell. I purposely skipped houses with blue Volvos. Both Mr. Shapiro, math, and Mrs. Sherwood, social studies, had blue Volvos and were proud to be teachers. I scouted for UFT stickers and any other symbols of teacherdom. Can you imagine? "Why Denzel, what are you doing?" You, as in class valedictorian. You, as in product of one of our better Black families.

I sold a few, but I lost a lot. The new pitch wasn't working and it was too late to pull out my old standby, Dinizulu, and maintain his accent with some credibility. I glanced Mello's way to see how he was doing, hoping he could throw me a little incentive. He had his own problems.

Mello stopped at a pay phone on the next corner. Within seconds he was yelling *"¡Mira, bruja!"* into the receiver. Judging from his crazed expression, she must have hung up on him. Mello took the receiver and slammed it against the pay box a few times.

The *bruja* could have been only one female—Ymangila. His other girls fought one another. Ymangila fought him. Rumor had it she was teaching her son to call some other dude *papi*, and that the other dude bought her a stroller.

I wanted to say something but held back. Leave him alone, I thought. The man was wild and was sure to confuse me with his problems.

After ranting to himself and kicking concrete, he seemed to get back on the trail, making some kind of resolve. He came to a green house where a guy was doing yard work. He was a young guy, with a brown ponytail and no shirt, but was hardly a kid. They started talking—definitely not about Miss Minerva's Cookies and Nutty Crunch. Mello took something out of his back pocket. They went around to the side of the house. A few minutes passed. Mello came out a whole new guy.

I see and I don't see.

We continued down the block. I gave up fighting my perspiration with a soaked handkerchief. The sun hadn't even reached its high point and it was killing us. We wouldn't last the remaining five hours. I sold three, a sorry number, and Mello's second wind had fallen flat. He sold five—four to the long-haired guy at the green house—and now he was pushing his case even slower.

Weber would be driving through soon, trying to turn things around with that phony smile and pep talk. He could talk major league pitching until October. It was too hot to care about skimming donations, High Man, or selling an honest can. We were in Queens, of all places. Grizzly old men with funky dentures giving me advice. People whom I'd never let close a screen door on me wouldn't even come to their doors. This had to be how Bad and Shawanda felt every day of their sorry lives. Shut out on face value. Not even given half a chance. Just get the hell away from my door.

My case never bothered me before. Today it weighed me down. My carrying hand hurt. The cardboard handle cut grooves into my palm. I found myself switching hands, stopping to soothe them. I wasn't used to carrying a loaded case for more than a few minutes. I came this close to dropping it— dropping everything. The only thing left to do was to fold up shop and call it a loss.

I got Mello's attention and gave him the signal to pack it in. "Let's track Mikie, Bad, and Shawanda and get the heck out of Dodge. It's time, man."

"Been time," Mello said, crossing over to my side.

We caught Mikie at the avenue. He had sold twelve and didn't want to stop selling. "Let me clean out this block and I'll meet you up ahead." It figured. Mikie was High Man. He had four to sell before finishing his case and wasn't quitting until he did.

We went looking for Bad and Shawanda. It didn't take much to find them. Search for a rain cloud, and underneath you'll find Shawanda and Bad. See the suspects disturbing the peace, and there are Shawanda and Bad.

Kew Gardens was no place to be with Shawanda or Bad. They frightened people who were home alone. One such person called in the neighborhood security force to investigate us. Three times the same black jeep crawled on our heels, observed, then drove by, probably to the next two streets where Bad, Shawanda, and Mikie were. Each time the driver radioed in, no doubt confirming that he had the suspicious gang under surveillance and needed backup. The third time I waved at him slow and friendly so he could see all five of my fingers. He didn't know what to make of a gesture that was supposed to be universal, and spit something back into the radio. He was pale, nervous. He had stumbled upon outlaw poachers carrying stolen goods, prowling for more, and there he was, armed with a nightstick, cuffs, and authority he didn't seem to want.

Great. What had Bad and Shawanda done this time? Probably said something so deep in Liberty Avenue talk that the customer mistook "Buy some, please" for "Hand over all your cash." It figured. What the good people of Kew Gardens called a reason to alert security was what we had grown used to as Bad Area Bob and Shawanda's mating ritual.

Sure enough. We found them three blocks behind the pace trading insults. They lugged their cases like they were carrying lead, which meant neither of them had sold a box, but both would have an alibi.

"Bad area, man. No tale, no sale." Bad grunted, dropped his case, and wiped his version of hard-earned sweat.

"Not one?" I asked.

"What can I tell you? The area's jinxed," Bad said.

"Yeah, right," Mello jumped in. "I sold five." Mello didn't like Bad. Not that Bad had ever done anything to Mello. Mello just didn't like Bad.

Then I added that I had sold three, and made sure to glare at Bad in disgust. Although the day was pointless and Bad wasn't expected to sell, it helped to have a target when things were messed up, and Bad was everybody's target.

"Aw, yaw had easy houses," Bad said with that sloppy grin, realizing A) he sounded stupid and B) he looked stupid. "Now take that first block I was in. Chief of police and whatnot. Then two diabetics, back to back—and one of them was kosher. It just wasn't in the cards. Nothing I could do. Bad area."

"Don't listen to him. He's a loser," Shawanda said. But by the sound of her heavy dropping box you knew that she was one too. "Bad, I'm tradin' you in. You just can't handle it."

"Whatchoo think? I'm your bodyguard and whatnot?" Then Bad cursed and spat. This was something he seldom did, and never in front of or at a female because it warped his self-image as a lover and detracted from his otherwise animated performances. "Every time I try to ease into my pitch, I look up and there's dust flying from 'cross the street 'cause you gettin' tough with the customers, 'specting me to strongman my way in there and drag you out.

"Dig this." Bad drew in some saliva to start his tale. "The lady tell Shwanna she not interested, which, if it were me I'da just said 'Cool' and kept walking. No. Shwanna start insulting her hair color and whatnot. Said she should save her two dollars to get her roots touched up. Then the lady say at least she don't got snakes growing out her head and 'fore you know it I gotta make like O.J., hurdle over a fence, and come pull Shwanna out of that lady yard. Lady had a dog, too. A big old dog. Here, Brutus. Kill, Brutus." Bad caught his breath and pointed to Shawanda because he couldn't make a declaration or tell a tale without synchronized movement. "As sure as I bleed true blood from a true heart, my insurance don't cover this."

Wise up, Bad. The funny papers was gonna get you, man. Pen you down in loud colors and make you a comic strip. "So why *didn't* you sell?" I asked.

"I told you why," he said. "I be all shot up behind Shwanna and her nonsense. Can't sell a free box to a hongry man all 'cuzza Shwanna stink attitude be dragging mines down and I be through for the day."

Shawanda shifted her hip and hand position three times, shaking her head and preparing her defense. "Me? My attitude drag you down? What about you? Shwanna, my box is heavy. I'm 'bout to break my back. Shwanna, I'm thirsty. Sell something quick so we can buy a soda. Shwanna, I gotta pee and these people won't let me in they house.

"Have you ever heard so much whining and crying? My baby brother don't holler so much and he only two. And that's

83

why you still got sixteen cans in that case. 'Cause you walking up to people door all sorry-eyed and slow-lipped, begging. So don't go blaming me for your sorry hard luck stories."

It was Bad's turn. "Listen up, guys," he said, stretching his jaws wide so you could see all the gold in his mouth. "I was set to unload a big sale. I had this lady so spellbound she was going to just give me her purse. Then Shwanna blows everything. Now I ask you. Could you sell if you had something like her throwing off your karma?"

"Karma? Who she? That skinny broad you tried to rap to? Well I don't want you either. Why? 'Cause you ain't a man, Bad. You got to have the muscle to protect this here," she said, making it obvious she was eyeing Mello. "And since you don't, I know who duz."

"Shawanda, don't even try it," I said, speaking up for my partner. Not that they could hear anything but their own squawking. Shawanda was just trying to get Bad on a slow burn.

"Mello, Mello. All the girls want Mello," Bad complained.

"Hey, it's like that," Mello bragged. "I got the juice."

"Hear dat, Shwanna? Mello got the juice. Won't you go get you some?" Bait taken.

"Look at you. Can't even say my name. It not Shwanna, all tired and slow like you say it. It Sha-wan-DA!"

"I know your story," Bad teased.

"What's my story?" Shawanda dared him to expose her.

Bad sang, "I know what's eating you."

Shawanda responded the only way she knew how. She took out a can of Nutty Crunch and wound up like she was going for Bad Area Bob's head.

Bad got tough, standing with his arms folded. He was a genie. Mr. Clean with one eyebrow raised, saying, "I wish you would."

The can made a metallic *bonk* sound off Bad's crown. Bad didn't move. He was in shock.

"Aw, see. Why'd you do that?" Bad weaved in semicircles like a Chinese parade dragon dodging firecrackers. "I know I said do it but that don't mean do it."

Shawanda and Bad took their argument up the street and across the overpass. We lagged behind because we had heard it all before and it was getting pretty old.

We approached the overpass. Cars sped underneath us on the highway. I avoided looking straight down because looking made me feel the impact of the drop. Every overpass in Queens was fortified with ten-foot-high chicken wire. This one, the one that I was crossing, had been neglected. The only guard on either side of the overpass was a four-foot iron railing.

I stayed to the far left of the sidewalk, away from the view of the highway, because heights always bothered me. When we were six, Cousin Randy and I schemed to get apples from Nana's tree in Brooklyn. Grampa Louis was alive then, and used to tell us about the sweet apples on the top branches. That was that. Had to have those sweet apples. Not to eat them, but to get them. We went up to the third floor of the brownstone and concocted a plan to get those sweet apples. Now, there was about two feet between the tree and the window. Since my arms were longer I did the reaching while Randy tied a sheet around my belt and hooked it up to Nana and Grampa's solid oak bed in case he got tired of holding me down. If I extended too far and found myself all the way out the window, no sweat. Randy would work the sheet like a pulley. The plan was foolproof. I plucked five apples, passing them inside to Randy. After raiding that first branch I inched out on the windowsill until I was practically in the tree. Then over to my right I saw an apple, bigger than the ones I had already picked, so I ventured out farther, angling myself into a better position when something unexpected happened. I looked down.

Mello didn't have a problem with heights, which came as no surprise. He was attracted to the twenty-foot drop and stopped to lean against the railing. "Look down there. Cars doing eighty. It's beautiful."

"I pass."

Mello was leaning over the railing, gazing down at the one-way traffic on the Grand Central. I was waiting for him to move on, but he wouldn't budge. He looked like he wanted to say something but instead said, "Skip it." Next thing I knew, Mello was throwing his leg over the rail. Then his other leg. His body went over. All I saw were two knobs of flesh holding onto vertical bars.

Out of nervousness I laughed at him and shouted, "Get your Tarzan swinging self up here!"

"Dig the view from here. It's beautiful." His voice was shaky and broken. He didn't sound like the Man of Steel. I took a few steps to the rail but never really looked down.

"Dig the view from here, Mello. You're looking like a dead man."

"Feel these cars under me . . . Wheeee. Can I hang, man?"

"Yeah, man. You can hang."

This was great. Just great. Mello got high 364 days out of the year without doing serious damage to himself. He would have to pick today to get high, act stupid, maybe even die, and make me see it, up close and in color. Just great.

I took another step toward him. The last thing I wanted to do was lean over the rail or look down on the highway. My stomach couldn't handle it. I'd lose it all over Mello's head, which would be justified—and on top of everything, I had to be the one to come up with a plan.

"I don't appreciate this, Mello. Makin' me a witness," I said, hoping he'd snap out of it, realize where he was, and pull himself up on his own. I wasn't even sure if he heard me. He was swinging like an ape. I was getting burnt so I yelled, "Jump, why don't you! It's not exactly a great suicide leap. Most you do is break a leg if you don't get hit by a car."

Mello started laughing. I couldn't tell if he was laughing at me, which meant he was okay, or if he was laughing at something else, which meant he was going to jump.

"Hey, man, can I hang or what?" he answered in that strange way.

I knew I had to look down so I aimed for the top of Mello's head. He shifted right and my eyes hit the highway. My heart made a lunge for my throat but got stuck in my chest. I saw myself falling, taking six Fs, eleven Ds, and eight Cs down with me. Things I had said and done passed before me. There was nothing I could do to take them back. Aw, man. That was a sure sign of dying, but I wasn't ready. I tried to yell for help, but my jaw was frozen. Bad and Shawanda were out there, but where? I couldn't even turn my neck to look for them. I could only look down and hear cars rolling loud, louder, loudest, then fading. My eighth-grade teacher once said, "Very good, Denzel," when I answered that this was what was known as the Doppler effect. I knew a lot of things, yet it only took a second for them to pass in front of me. None of these things would throw my luck back over the rail.

Mello was looking down from a twenty-foot drop talking about how beautiful it was to feel a breeze rushing you at top speed. I was looking down at a dead man. A dead man. As sure as I was standing there turning green, he was going to drop and get hit by a speeding truck, and I was going to be the one to see it all.

"Come on," I managed to say, very calmly, very evenly. "Come on, Mello."

Mello performed three rigid chin-ups. Motorists honked their horns, seeing his dangling feet. His attempt to spit smacked him in the face. He didn't care and made a sideways swinging motion to the next bar. He missed and was one-handing it.

I gripped the rail and offered him my hand, praying he wouldn't take it. "Come on, Mello."

Then IT happened. IT was in his face. He saw IT just like I had. He knew how high off the ground he was and that he was going to die. We looked each other in the eye and became joined by what we saw. I had never looked into a dead man's eye. Had he dropped and splattered on the highway, I'd have his eye in my face.

The spaciness was washed from his face. He clenched his teeth so every vein in his neck showed. Mello had decided he was stupid. He liked breathing air, screwing girls, and eating two and a half squares a day. He reached between the bars and grabbed my ankle with his gargantuan hand. His grip brought me dead into the rail. His weight was more than I could counter—physics should have told me that before I went offering my support like some kind of hero. I tried to hold on, but I was no match against the enormous pull of his lifeless body. My head, shoulders, and chest were being forced over the rail by a dead man.

Not I.

I let out a scream that was supposed to be a yell for help, but at this point I was dying. Who cared what it sounded like?

Bad heard my scream and came running.

Shawanda yelled for him to come back. "I'm not finished with you, fool."

Bad latched onto my back to help pull me up. Shawanda was right about Bad. He had no muscle, but he was all I had. I was regaining some leverage. Mello got a better grip on the rail and let go of my leg, which was either fractured or broken from being crushed by his hand. As though he didn't need our help to begin with, Mello climbed up the bar and pulled himself over like an Olympian, then toppled us. Bad got the squashed side of the deal.

Mello leaped up and danced around like a shadow boxer. "You simp! Screaming like a baby for your mama. Ah hah!" He laughed and continued to dance in circles. His face was bright and filled with blood. "Did you see what I saw, man? Did you see it? It was beautiful!" Mello exclaimed.

Yeah, I saw IT.

Bad went back to Shawanda, who was still fussing at the end of the overpass. I was down for the count. Mello was throwing straight, hard punches in the air, jerking his head left and right, taunting his monster to come at him. He threw a real hard one and waited for the counter punch. He dodged it and laughed.

"Can I hang? Can I hang, man?"

LOVE AND OTHER HAZARDS

Mello and Bad made limping a victory march, like a dancing tight end who comes up with ball in hand after taking a hard hit in the end zone. The only thing missing was six points and a reason for Mello's stunt.

Looking at Mello, you'd never know something had happened. He was laughing and talking about other things. Unimportant things. A new pair of sneakers he wanted to buy. Did they come in double-E width? Stuff like that.

Mello had simply dusted himself off and moved on. They all seemed farther away than they actually were—maybe because I could hardly move. But what to do first? Take a step? Breathe? Think? Breathing made my ribs sore. Thinking made my head buzz. That left movement. I worked my joints mechanically and let out a low groan so they couldn't hear me hurting. It was worse than I thought so I stood in one spot pretending to survey the distance to the pick-up point.

Mello and Bad amazed me. I couldn't fake a crawl, and they were shadowboxing and clowning. Two minutes ago I was on the edge of my life, Mello was at the end of his, and now he was talking about finding checkered laces for sneakers he didn't even own.

Not that I didn't understand, because I did. Talking about it would have been as uncool as blowing a roulette spin between you and an oncoming car as you were crossing the street. You didn't walk faster, leap onto the sidewalk, or acknowledge that the speeding car wanted your life. No. You just kept striding, slowed it down if you were really good, and didn't think about it twice when you crossed the street.

Understanding it didn't mean I was with it. I felt myself exploding. Talk about being scared white, watching my life going over the rail. I couldn't leave it alone. I had to ask Mello if it was a dare, a spur-of-the-moment bad idea, or if he was trying to do something.

When I looked up I saw that Mikie had joined the crew and I wondered if they were going to fill him in. Mikie seemed to fall into whatever it was they were laughing about, and they continued to move farther away, talking about irrelevant things. Based on that, I could assume no one would turn around to see if I was okay. The best thing to do was catch up, blend in, shut up.

Weber came quick to hustle us out of the area. I wouldn't be surprised if the security patrol tipped off the real police anonymously to avoid dealing with us, a wild bunch of "ghetto" kids. Two blue and white patrol cars came with sirens blasting as we rounded the corner and headed for the Grand Central Parkway. It didn't matter how far down the Grand Central we drove, I was going to smell tar for the rest of the day.

As expected, the crew carried on dully, waiting for something big to happen. Mikie sat up front counting his earnings from Kew Gardens. Shawanda and Bad sat together, spit flying back and forth. I sat in the back with Mello, who was laughing to himself about the view from a twenty-foot drop.

We merged into the narrow single lane of the Interboro, and headed for Brooklyn—which is what we should have done in the first place.

Weber was disgusted. Collectively we had made less than fifty dollars. Seeing that the money had to be divided among Jack, Weber, and us, it had been a wasted day. Weber, however, refused to chalk up the loss. This was clear as he pressed the gas pedal.

"Everyone hits a slump now and then. Ya gotta prove you're above it. And what's the best way to accomplish that?" he quizzed as though we were sitting in a classroom dying to be called on. "Get right back out there and sell," he answered, brown eyes jumping from the rearview mirror to his watch, the sun, and occasionally the snaky road.

To show how much he cared, he headed for the East New York section of Brooklyn. Every-man-for-himself territory. We weren't worth the extra gas to Brooklyn Heights or Sheepshead Bay, where housewives with pantries as big as bank vaults lay waiting to be cajoled out of diets. No. Throw us where we'll have to watch our backs, look over our shoulders, find some sharp object, and dash like quicksilver. So much for beating a slump.

Boxes shifted from side to side as the van leaned heavily into the curves of the road. At the next sharp curve Bad put his weight into Shawanda's side. She punched his shoulder. He retaliated with a coyote howl in her ear, wounding her more than her punch did him. It was probably killing her to know that her fist wasn't deadly enough to keep Bad in line. Bad, feeling victorious, had exposed Shawanda as a big phony. All lip and no hit.

Mikie put down his millions and asked Shawanda what her problem was. The "nuffin'" she grumbled was low and muddy. Bad stuck his finger under her chin, knowing what was eating her up. Shawanda grabbed his hand and slapped it so hard dust flew from his ashy fingers. Bad's spirit rose higher and he let go another coyote howl along with the secret that had Shawanda on edge. "Shwanna got a sister."

"A sister?" Mikie was surprised for the same reason we all were. Shawanda's home stories always included battles with six brothers. A sister was never mentioned.

"Not just a sister. A twin!"

"Two Shawandas? Holy earthquake!"

"Watch it, little man," Shawanda snapped, pointing her finger. Bad might be feeling adventurous, but Mikie had better not try it. Shawanda had him by a good fifty pounds. He chuckled and went back to his dollar bills.

Since Bad had lost Mikie as his audience, he turned to Mello and me. "Wanna hear how her name go?"

Shawanda hissed. Bad grinned. "Shaneequa. Just as sweet as she is." He closed his eyes to taste what he was dreaming. Shawanda's face darkened.

The more I tried to picture them together, the more hysterical their image became. Before I knew it I had jumped in as Bad's accomplice and was snapping on Shawanda. "Isn't there a one-to-a-planet limit on your species?" I asked. She ignored me. "Where ya been hiding her, Wanda?" I asked louder, hoping to draw a little blood.

"Shawanda. It Shawanda!" she insisted. "Bad can't say my

name without his lips gettin' in the way—now you gotta go cuttin' me off. Wanda. Who that? This here is Shawanda."

Bad was too willing to volunteer details about Shawanda's missing half. "She visiting from down souf. Ain't seen her yet but I swear she sweet. It's in her voice." As always, his hands told the story, accompanying it with a beat. "I was on the phone calling Godzilla when I hear this voice. Man! Sweet like I never heard it. Almost went into shock. Had to hang up. Redial. And there is sweetness saying, 'Hello, this is Shaneequa. Can I help you?' " He mimicked the voice and rolled his eyes. Bad was a clown. He couldn't help himself. He sang, taking his vocal talents too seriously, "Shaneequa got the sweetness."

"Coulda been me," Shawanda sulked.

"Dip your tongue in honey and that still wouldna been you. Lick a all-day sucker and that still wouldna been you. Ummph! Bet yo' sister truly fine."

"We twins, fool. Look the same, sound the same." Shawanda folded her arms in her lap. She was fighting tears, and Bad didn't have sense enough to leave it alone.

"You two twins like I'm Chinese," Bad rubbed it in. "A minute on the phone and I can tell diamonds from hard rock. Shaneequa got that sparkle. And you a rock, Shwanna."

Shawanda was biting down hard on her lip. Bad had her pinned tight. If she spoke her mask would crumble in her lap, and Shawanda couldn't have that. She had lost everything else. She couldn't lose her face.

"Umm, umm. Shaneequa, the sweet one. When you gonna bring her around? Can't wait to meet her face to face. Take her out. Spend some real money on her. She from down souf, too! They grow them like peaches down souf. Big, red and yellow, and sweet. The sweetest girls you wanna know 'bout."

Then Mello leaned forward and stroked one of Shawanda's

braids. "Shawanda sweet," he said in her ear. "Shawanda real sweet."

Shawanda was one grateful female. Her stone mask gave way to the impossible. Impossible because of her nature, not her shade. Shawanda blushed.

Mello turned her chin with his thumb so he could lay that stare on her. He winked, pretending to know something Bad didn't, and added, "Believe that."

Everything got quiet. Bad stopped performing.

Weber slowed down, circling our area three blocks east and six blocks south. He indicated the pickup point and threw in a diluted pep talk, emphasizing that he would be cruising every half hour to give us encouragement, which immediately translated to us exactly how he meant it. He'd be watching us to see why we weren't making money.

Had Weber taken into consideration our poor locale and the oppressive sun, he'd know we were defeated from the start. Weber couldn't have cared less about causes. He was only concerned with selling. As long as there were still three hours left to the working day, we had to push boxes, defeated or not.

Shawanda didn't feel defeated. She was agitated, anxious, and had to do something about it. Not even the mention of her sister's name would make a dark rain cloud appear. It was all because of Mello.

It never failed. Instead of being sore with Mello for endangering my life, I was studying him, wondering what it would be like to have his kind of weight.

Not a kiss, sterling silver rap, or a piece of jewelry. But because *he* said so, Shawanda was transformed, feeling good about herself! Why? Because Mello knew three, maybe four words—and one-syllable words at that. "Shawanda sweet. Shawanda real sweet." Geez. If there was any sport to this, I'd do the same thing for Bad, just to keep things even between Mello and me.

Weber discharged Bad and Shawanda first, and gave them a warning. I watched them from the van.

Shawanda took off, face lit up, eager to sell to her customers. She added a smile to her pitch and sold to her first house. As if that weren't enough, she said something after making the sale which could have been a "thank you."

Bad was mad. I could see air escaping from his big balloon head. His box was heavy and destined to get heavier. He dropped it and kicked it to his next house. Seeing he was having a rough day, the woman in the yard went into her pocket without hearing his pitch. He was so awful that she kept her hand and her money in her pocket.

His cardboard case got another hard kick. For one moment Bad had had Shawanda on his terms. He could have become her protector after having crushed her flat because that was what it took to win a girl like Shawanda, who threw her brothers around like plywood. She'd have no choice but to look up and see that he was a knight, too. But just before he was supposed to remind her who had whose chain, then mercifully cut her some slack, yank! Mello took it all away. Once again, Bad was a six-foot-one-inch punk asking who, what, and how, when it was all too late.

When was Bad gonna wake up? Love did terrible things to his face. His lip was hitting bottom, it was so heavy. He never could straighten his spine before. Now he was concave to the world and was reduced to kicking his cardboard case, the only thing that couldn't kick back—that is, if you didn't count the fact that its fullness branded him a loser.

Occasionally he'd glance at her, wondering what happened, especially with victory being so close. He threw a rock at her, hoping she'd shoot him down with her tongue or throw a can of Crunch upside his head. Shawanda dodged the rock and didn't give Bad a second thought. She was singing sweetly and not caring to hide it. Probably Mello's name. Next thing you knew, she'd start coming in wearing perfume and acting all stink.

It was going to take more than three one-syllable words to turn Bad's luck around. I couldn't even further my own cause. My pitch was dull, and at this point I couldn't care less. Then I ran into, or up against, *her*.

"Let me get this straight," said she, a girl my age, whose whistling articulation had the annoyance of chalk on a blackboard. Oh, I had her read. Plaid skirts didn't lie. She was one of those Blacks who practiced the *s* and *th* sounds, making sure the tongue did all of the right things. "You're selling this garbage as part of you college scholarship?" she interrogated, while examining Miss Minerva's ingredients. Also, she was ugly. Black crayon ugly and forceful about it.

"Yes, miss," I answered, just short of meekness, hoping to disarm her skepticism. Sometimes people back off when they realize they're being unnecessarily tough. "For every box or can that I sell I'll receive matching scholarship funds to Princeton this fall."

"Well I'm going to Yale on full scholarship." Screech. "Academic scholarship." Screech. "Couldn't you get an academic scholarship?" Screech. Screech.

Hey, D, smack the bitch.

"Well?" (And her glasses were blinding me, too.)

"Miss, does it really matter how I get to Princeton? Even Malcolm X—you've heard of Malcolm X?—was fond of preaching 'by any means necessary.' So what does it matter if I get to Princeton on a full scholarship, or by selling cookies, or with an M-16 in my hand? The point is that I'll get there." Hearing Vernon's words fire from my mouth cut short my gloating. I was amazed and sickened by the realization that Vernon's propaganda was glued to my subconscious.

"Of course I meant—"

"Nothing by that? Funny. That's usually what *they* say." I played it up, shaking my head mournfully. That's right, girl. Look stupid.

"Well, here's two dollars but keep the candy. I hope I have contributed to your education." Spoken like a true female. Had to get the last lick and close the door quickly to assure a victory. Had to let me know that she was going to Yale. Of course she had to. Who else could she have shared that bit of info with? I was still one up on her. She had no idea she was headed for a nosedive when she got to Yale.

I waved over to Mello. *"Sellin?"* *"So-so."* Normally I'd start breaking on his technique as a preface to a friendly game of High Man Draw or Fair Game. But neither of us was sufficiently motivated to play those games. We were both averaging one sale to a block and hadn't even thought about skimming donations.

I told Mello we had two more blocks to go when we both heard a loud pop, which could have been a blown tire, an exploding ash can, or a gunshot. We would have gone on about our business except we heard Shawanda hollering, "Mikie! Mikie!"

Mello dropped his case and took off in the direction of Shawanda's voice. I went across the street and picked up Mello's case, a good excuse for arriving late to the scene. The last thing I wanted to do was arrive in time to help Mello tussle with some gun-heavy thugs. Mello already had a slug mark on his back, just below his shoulder. It was no big thing to him. He was just looking to add another bullet wound to his body, whereas I wanted to live.

When I got there, Mello was kneeling over Mikie, who was

crying about his money. I fell into the small circle of spectators to see what was what. Good. No body parts. No heavy bleeding. Just Mikie writhing on the sidewalk, holding his ears. His case had been ripped apart. There were boxes of Miss Minerva's cookies and cans of Crunch all over the street.

"They wanted my money. My money! I didn't give it up, though. They took it," he added, as though he had to make that clear.

"You did good, Mikie," Mello said. He picked up Mikie's tiny body and laid him down on the hood of the nearest parked car. Mikie shivered despite the heat. Damn. He was so little. No man should have to be that little.

Mello turned to me. "I say we get 'em and duke 'em up. They couldn't even shoot him like a man. Let's go!"

Mello was serious.

Bad backed away. I should have done the same thing, but I couldn't. Instead, I made corroborating noises like I was down.

Shawanda picked the glass out of Mikie's wounds. She dusted the street out of Mikie's hair and wiped the blood from his scraped forearms with her tee shirt. Her firm handling seemed to calm Mikie's shaking, although he wouldn't let go of his ears.

Mello asked Mikie what they looked like. What colors was the guy wearing who had the gun? What direction did they go?

Before he could cough, Shawanda put her hand over Mikie's mouth and asked, "Why? So you can kill yourself for real? Just thank God they missed his ear. They was aiming for his head."

I could see Weber's van approaching. I was grateful he kept his promise to stick close, especially with Mello giving orders to split up and go after the guys who stole Mikie's money.

Shawanda didn't let the van come to a complete stop. She went straight for the driver's window and started beating on the glass, yelling, "See what you did! Stuck us in the jungle and see!" She pointed to Mikie spread out on the car. "If it wasn't for Mello we'd have no protection."

Mikie rode up front, lamenting his stolen money yet making it clear that they *took* it. Mello and Shawanda sat in the middle seat, arm in arm. I got stuck in the back with Bad, who was not beneath crying over Shawanda.

Shawanda, with her entire case sold, was High Man for the day. Mikie would have been High Man if he hadn't gotten ripped off. Mello and I were about tied, with eight and nine pieces sold. Bad had sold one.

No one hung around the office like we usually did. We all walked to the train station in staggered pairs. Mikie was supposed to go to the emergency room with Shawanda, but he walked ahead and disappeared. Bad, who always walked with Shawanda, lagged several paces behind the new couple. Mello made it clear that he now *had* Shawanda, and if Bad wanted her, which he did, he'd have to wait. Mello pulled Shawanda closer. Whatever he whispered made her eyes reach up to his and stay there. Mello and Shawanda stopped walking, so Bad stopped. Mello took his time kissing her while Bad just stood there waiting for them to finish.

Happy, Shawanda went down into the station. Bad followed her. Mello and I lingered at the top of the stairs.

"Shawanda?" I asked Mello.

"She okay. Rock solid outside. Sweet inside," he said. "Gila's like that." Gila. Mello's magic word. One minute she was a witch, the next minute she was candy.

He pushed up his sleeve to show off marks on his skin, apparently made by fingernails. Had to be Ymangila's. He traced them carefully, not because the wounds were still tender, but because the streaks had meaning. "She's got poison. See how it got all infected," he said, shoving his scarred arm in my face. I stepped back, but he wouldn't take the hint, keeping his arm in my face. "Look at it, man." He beamed.

That kind of admiration flew right by me, but Mello was one illogical dude. Nothing Mello did made sense, least of all why he had bailed Shawanda out at Bad's expense.

"Bad's a punk. He should have kicked my ass. But what did he do? Nothing. I'da half respected him if he hit me. Mouthed off. Stood up for his woman. Something."

"Sure, sure. Anything you say, Jay."

"S'pose it was your girl I was kissing. You'da just stood there looking stupid?"

"Mello, you couldn't get to my girl," I boasted, knowing she didn't exist. "You couldn't get to my baby sister, so squash that talk."

"D, your girl, your sister, and your mother." He laughed. "A skirt's a skirt."

Didn't I cough in his face? Lydia didn't own a skirt like that. Lydia, and even Kerri for that matter, were both untouchable. Everything in my house was untouchable and immune to Mello's charisma. I didn't even bother to counter his off-the-wall crack.

Then, out of the blue, as we were both watching a pack of really young girls marching up from the subway, he said, "Statutory. What's dat?" He was bothered by the word, although he tried to hide it.

"It means she's a minor, but don't sweat it. So are you."

"Hey. I don't have to be statuing no girl against her word. Not when I got girls throwing it at me."

It didn't sound wrong the way he said it. It sounded like statuing a girl was something you did to her. Turned her into stone. I liked that, so I didn't bother to correct him.

He looked worried. "She got the court sending papers to my house, man. Long papers. Deep papers. My moms hit the roof. Told me I was gonna get locked up again, and that's what I get for messing with poison. Locked up, man. Can you believe that?"

I answered, "Naw," playing it on his side. He kept saying "locked up" over and over. Even I was getting scared for him.

"What I can't figure out is why she's doing this. She think it's funny," he said, banging his head against the handrail. "Dig this. She calls my house last night and says, 'You get my love letter?' like it's a joke."

"Think she'll take you to court?" I asked.

"Nah," he said confidently, not fooling anyone though. "She's into voodoo. Loves sticking pins in me. I get her. She gets me back. Dig this. She sayin' Rafael ain't even mines. I cried when she told me that shit. I hate her, man."

"That's deep," I sympathized. Mello cried. I wished he hadn't told me that. Not that it fazed him none to tell me he cried. He shrugged it off and kept talking.

He was depressing me. I couldn't take it. I had to change the subject. I suggested we hang out one night after collecting our pay. Wreak havoc all over Manhattan like the old times. He seemed mildly interested, but he still wanted to talk about his problems as though I had all the answers. All I knew at that moment was that I wanted to get away from Mello and go home. "Well, yeah, man. I hear what you're saying. We'll speak on that later," I promised, going down the stairs, thinking, if he makes it to tomorrow.

Mello, Ymangila, Bad, Shawanda, and Mello again. Everyone riding high, then low, getting sick to their stomachs, hanging over highways, lying, crying, and turning into stone. If this was love I wasn't taking a fall no time soon. *She* just didn't exist. But, if she did, I'd be quick to get insurance. A cushion to fall back on. Like, she'd have to love me more than I loved her, but she couldn't hang onto me like I was a basic life function.

The train wasn't moving fast enough. I was looking forward to being home and enjoying the quiet, some dinner, TV. I even wanted to see my family, although I couldn't exactly explain why. They hated my summer job. If they knew what happened today they'd make me quit, and I wasn't ready to do that.

Unfortunately, Lydia wasn't going to let this be a nice evening at home. She started up the minute I put the key in the door. *Yang yang yang.* Did it really matter what she was saying? *Yang yang yickety yang yang.* Something about my dorm reservation and I was past deadline. *Yangety yang yang.* I'd be sitting in the Commons with my suitcase if she hadn't come to the rescue. *Yang yang yang.* Son, you're a college man. Let's act like one.

I had one thing on my side. Lydia wasn't going through my drawers, because if she was, she would have found a stack of unopened mail from Princeton. I'd have to explain myself and all hell would break loose. But after Mello hanging, bullets flying, and battling the ugly Yalie, a little home static seemed trivial. I cleared my throat several times during the dinner discussion. The minute I said *Princeton,* Lydia and Vernon relived college days, all the while working in my dual roles as firstborn son and Black man on campus, like I was the spokesman for my race to the planet Zutonia. I knew I didn't try hard enough to tell them, but they'd get the picture when they saw that I hadn't packed in September.

The next day Shawanda had sense enough not to be buzzing around Mello. She was wearing a dress and was trying to talk a little different, as though her twin were giving her lessons.

She proclaimed this a "new day," declaring herself a serious contender for High Man. For good luck she gave a box of cookies to some kids playing in the street.

"I don't know why you're doing all of that. Mello gots him so many girls he don't even notice."

"Mello?" She looked surprised, and then grinned at Bad. "It ain't for Mello."

"Then who? I want to know."

"Fool."

"Aw, Shwanna. You give them kids some candy. What you got for me?"

Old Shawanda jumped out. "I thought I didn't have no candy. Not even if I dipped my tongue in honey or licked an all-day sucker." Then she sighed, becoming "soft" Shawanda again, seeming to enjoy her ability to change and be any kind of Shawanda she felt like.

"Aw, Shwanna. Don't be like that."

Shawanda walked away from Bad, saying, "Fool, fool, fool. You blew, blew, blew."

I sold out my case of cookies and looked for Bad to make a switch. When Weber didn't come fast enough to replenish the stock you could always count on Bad to have loads of everything. At the very least he was a pack mule. When I found him, he was still sporting that wounded animal look, toting his heavy, unsold case.

"How's it selling, Bad?"

"Bad area. No tale, no sale. It's like that sometimes."

"Shawanda looks like she's doing okay," I pointed out.

"Yeah, and I wish she'd cut it out."

"Bad, you're pathetic."

"What? Me?"

"She know you like her. Who don't know that? She got you, nose wide open."

"She ain't right," was the best he could do in assessing his situation.

"Damn straight," I said, hoping to fire him up. "So what you gonna do about it?"

"Come clean," he said, putting his hands up to surrender.

"Bad, you disgust me. You can't let her get away with it. Know what you should do? Throw it back at her. Get someone. Anyone. Have her meet you on payday like you're taking her out. Play it up to Shawanda's face."

"No, no, no. I'm not Mello. I don't got lots of girls. I'm not you, D. I'm not the iceman. I can't live without having that feeling in my heart. When I love someone I got to let them know. I'm gonna lay it straight and say, 'Shwanna. You know you wants to be mines, so what you gonna do?'"

"Don't do it, man. Love can be hazardous to your health," I warned, knowing I had lost him, which was too bad. I could have rescued Bad from the funny papers. I could have done for Bad what Mello did for Shawanda. Two more minutes and Bad would have had some heart.

Bad dropped his case and walked over to Shawanda. He actually straightened his spine, walking tall to his doom. She must have known he was coming because she slowed down so he could catch her. He was going to croon like a canary. Already by his hand gestures and his side to side stepping, I sensed the return of the background singer, pleading his case.

She said something about her name. She was going to teach him to say her name. He was nodding like he was too eager to learn.

I couldn't watch. I bent down and helped myself to Bad's case. He certainly had no use for it.

PAYDAY DREAMING

SATURDAY was great. Even without Mikie we beat out Dave's crew, unloading ten cases to their six. It was payday and we were all in a good mood, sitting around the office talking big doo doo and payday dreaming. Bad was telling Shawanda about everything he was going to buy her with his thirty-eight dollars. Shawanda, to whom I had given more credit, was ecstatic. The two new crew members that Jack had hired were going to the movies after they got their pay. Mello and I finalized our plans to meet later and hang out in the city.

No one talked about Mikie or that it had been a week since we had seen him. We knew if Mikie didn't show on payday, that was as good as a swan song. All I knew was when I left— soon—they'd better talk about me for a month. Not just yawn like I was never a part of it.

"Let's split up Mikie's," Bad called out to Weber, who was doling out the envelopes. Bad was ignored.

Mello got his envelope. I was next. I felt the brown envelope from end to end. It was definitely fatter than Mello's. My High Man bonus had been issued in singles. I smiled at Jack and Weber's simplicity. I was supposed to think I had a lot more money because it was stacked higher. I was both amazed and insulted that they completely overlooked my style, thinking I was one of those tacky dudes who pulled out huge bankrolls to buy a comic book. The first thing I resolved to do was trade in the sloppy wad for six twenties.

Mello had his own accounting system. Every Saturday he took his pay, counted it up, and divided it three ways. The thickest stack was his rent money, which he paid his mother at the end of each week. No rent, no bed. The second pile went to Ymangila and her son. The third and thinnest stack was his. Sometimes there was a fourth one for some other girl and her kids, but that didn't happen too often.

Today Mello dispensed with the ritual. He pushed the bills down in his pocket without counting, and said, "Let's blow it all."

"Are you serious? Don't you have things to do?" I asked, at the risk of getting personal.

"Like what?"

"You know," I said, wishing I hadn't asked him anything. There are some bounds you don't cross, like *you mean your mother makes you pay to sleep there?* I'd never pay money to live at home. Vernon and Lydia owed me the world because they brought me into it. That's the way it should be. It didn't seem right that Mello had to pay rent to his own mother.

Mello said to forget about it. He had it all worked out.

Whenever he was short with his rent he stayed at the Newtown Arms, a state setup for teenage girls and their kids. He'd find a girl there, help her with her groceries or laundry, talk to her. Some attention and a box of Pampers usually got him all of the lodging he could stand. Soon he'd get bored, see another girl, and move on. It was a contest for the girls as well. Who would get Mello? Whose kids did he love most? Who could keep him longest? Mello went from floor to floor at the Newtown, causing problems. By the third day of his various stays, he'd have two girls clawing it out in front of their kids.

As long as he could remember, Carmello was forever making girls love him. They loved his darkness, his mood swings, and the idea that they were the cause. Girls easily dropped their guard for Mello. He had a daughter when he was thirteen, but lost track of her. He told me about some other kids scattered around Queens, but only called one of them by name—Rafael. The one whom Ymangila named after another guy just to get back at Mello.

If Mello was worried about the prospect of having no money, being locked up, or not having his rent, he kept it to himself. He had made up his mind that the money in his pocket was his alone. He didn't move or change expression when he heard her voice as she came up the stairs.

It was like bantam hens on a pecking mission. Ymangila marched ahead, a queen trailed by her sergeants at arms, who each had a grip on the stroller as they carried it up the stairs. Ymangila's sisters were cheering her on as she warmed up for her round with Mello.

She entered, head held high, attitude at the ready. She was even more beautiful than when I had seen her last year. Having that baby did not humble her in the least or dent her figure. She could still wear jeans and heels, and she knew it. Her hair was bright and firey with curls fluffed out and falling over her shoulders. Her makeup was perfection, not caked on in desperation. She obviously spent a lot of time putting herself together so she could drive him nuts while she threatened him.

Ymangila had her three-month-old son looking like a prince in a yellow outfit with matching cap, bib, and booties. His stroller was a top-of-the-line model with a sun net draped over it.

Mello was not impressed. He sat back, putting his feet up on the opposite bench. His arms stayed welded across his chest, and his eyes grew cold until he appeared numb.

The office got quiet. Ymangila and Mello's confrontations were always good shows, and no one wanted to miss a word. Ymangila started first. Rafael was low on formula. He needed to see the pediatrician and what was Mello going to do about it. Mello's response was that she had food stamps and Medicaid, and why should it matter to him since the kid wasn't his. She said you blind or stupid. Look at him and you know I lied. Mello said, "Those papers you sent to my house was a lie, 'cause I never forced you." She said her parents made her do that. And he said, "Yeah, baby. And I was born six two."

In his heart, Mello wasn't half as cold as he fronted, because ordinarily he would have given her the money with no fuss. He just couldn't bring himself to ask her to cut him some slack. It was easier for him to be cold.

Now I wished I hadn't edged him out of today's bonus. He was stretched too thin, and from keeping score I knew he couldn't have made more than eighty honest dollars, plus sixty in donations. Knowing Mello, his donations got blown along the way. He must have figured, since he didn't have both rent and Ymangila's money, no one was getting any.

I would have offered him the bonus, but he would've thought I was trying to chump him in front of his son's mother. And one thing I knew about Mello: You could snap on him, steal from him, or take a swing at him, and you'd still be okay to Mello. But don't disrespect him. Once that line was crossed, someone had to fall.

Carmello, being the Man of Steel, looked at the little boy and hated his yellow clothes on sight. He offered Ymangila a twenty-dollar bill and said, "That's what I got."

Ymangila didn't touch the money. Twenty dollars was not what she came for. "That don't buy clothes for him."

"All he needs is a tee shirt and a diaper. Stop doing him like some dress-up doll. He's a boy," Mello said.

"My son wears the best," Ymangila insisted.

"Look at this. Yellow. What are you trying to make him? You the mother. Act like it."

"That's right, I'm the mother. I take him to the doctor. I feed him. I go get his formula. I'm there when he's crying. I carry him around. What do you do?"

Come on, man. Throw her another twenty, I thought.

Mello stood up and went to inspect his son. Ymangila's sisters stood aside. I sincerely hoped Mello could handle those rough sisters. I prayed he wasn't looking for no backup. Those sisters watched Ymangila and their nephew as though they were sworn to protect them. Ymangila kept talking, but Mello was too busy eyeing the baby. The boy was big for a three-month-old. He had Mello's face, and he was being raised by a girl who both hated and loved Mello.

"I'm the mother and I need thirty more dollars," Ymangila demanded, spreading her long red nails that looked good up against Mello's bronze skin. "This here twenty dollars don't feed him or buy him clothes."

Mello must have heard me halfway through my silence and peeled out another ten. "That's all I got. There ain't no more."

Ymangila cursed Mello, the ten, and the twenty, but took the money all the same. She signaled her sisters to pick up the stroller, and they went down the stairs, cluck, cluck, clucking.

"Carmello's a good name. She could have called him that. My name is Carmello. Who knows? Maybe my father's name is Carmello," he said, wanting to believe that. I could tell he wanted things for Rafael but seemed powerless to do anything.

I looked away and said, "Carmello's an okay name. Not everyone has it."

"Why she does that? Come around. She gets welfare. Who does she think she is, coming up here with her bodyguards?"

I never knew what to say when Mello talked about her like he was seeking advice. Their relationship was wrapped up in Mello and Ymangila's ways of love and hate. If I were Mello, I would have left her a long time ago and said who needed it. But just like Mello was always griping about her, he wasn't letting go and she was the same way. Although she got more money from welfare than Mello could ever give her pushing cookies and candy, she wasn't letting go either.

"We still on, or are you tapped?"

"On."

"How are you gonna hang with a couple of dollars in your pocket, especially where we're going?"

"I'll get it."

"Look, Mello. If you can't fly first class, I'll dig you on the runway," I told him. "I don't want you embarrassing me, man. 'Yo, D, man, I'm short. Can you buy my date a drink?' "

He started laughing again, which was good because I was going to skip it if he didn't improve his outlook. He plucked me on the shoulder and said, "You know how it's gonna be? All right. I'll tell you. Picture this. Girls everywhere, opening their purses and knocking themselves out to make me happy. I mean, I could go with twenty-five cent and a token to get me home and I'll still come out ahead, unlike some poor stiffs who have to beg the girl to dance, buy drinks for her and her girlfriends, then get dumped."

"We'll see," I told him.

We split up to go home, get ready, and meet at the Jackson Heights station at ten. From there we'd ride into the city and hit spots where celebrities were known to hang out. Then the true contest would begin.

TWO BOYS, ONE KNIGHT

WHEN I got home I checked to see if I had any messages. As usual, there were none, or Kerri forgot to write them down.

The family had already eaten and was going out for the evening. Before Lydia could make the suggestion I reminded her I already had plans and would be getting in late, so don't chain the door. I started to ask for the second time if anyone had called, but was fast enough to stop myself. If she had something to say in the way of an apology she would have said it. And if I really cared, I would have left the door open for her to say something. Forget Wendy.

Tonight Mello and I were going for titles. Best Dressed. Best Rap. Most Cash. Most Cool. Best Girl. And that all-time coveted title, Best Steal. With the first three titles undeniably mine, the others were in the bag.

I had a flashy suit of armor lined up and waiting for me to jump into. Underwear with a signature. Nylon socks. Casually elegant loafers. Giorucci shirt. Smoke gray linen jacket with tuxedo lapels and matching pleated pants. The touch? A pure silk lavender bow tie.

Next, I put my wallet in order. I folded a twenty into a sharp square and placed it behind the ID that I had selected for the night. I had a credit card, eighty dollars to flash, forty to spend, cards with my phone number, cards with fake numbers, and an emergency rubber for Mello.

I got clean and suited up, then took that final spin in the mirror, convinced I could cut glass if I turned fast enough. I got on the bus to Jamaica Avenue so I would be near the 165th Street mall and the subway. There was still enough time for a trim and shape-up at the mall, so I made it before the barber shop closed. After that, I headed for the train, testing my appearance on girls who couldn't help but notice how good I looked.

The train ran local, which was fine because I didn't want to be too early. I arrived at Jackson Heights station with ten minutes to spare, looking forward to the classic confrontation between Mello and me and to watching his face say, "Uh-oh, check out the competition." I rocked back on my heels, savoring the moment, and thought the night wasn't falling fast enough.

This is what it was all about. True knights, charging at each other face to face and at our absolute best. Being in on each other's conquests to jeer or give a nod, cut or be cut, then ride home and add up the points. The swords. The fellowship. The girls, too, but they were just a part of it. Not *in* it. Then after everything was settled, Mello and I were still okay with each other, except only one knight was standing.

There was never any doubt who that would be. Even the gust

from the train pulling in on the opposite track blew in my favor, rustling through my clothing, making my silhouette dance with grace while I remained perfectly still. *Yeah. I be nicin'.*

Mello finally showed, wearing his pappy's wedding clothes. Black pants. White shirt. Black socks. Black shoes.

We dispensed with the greetings and took the next train to the city. I had to give it to Mello. He wasn't the least bit concerned that I outclassed him in the clothing division. But then, it wasn't exactly a surprise that I would.

We looked around the car to see if we could spot our prospective dates for the evening. So far nothing was happening. The women were biting, but not worth our interest. It was still amusing to give the four-point rating to the unsuspecting girls who entered the car. Face, legs, hair, and class.

Mello called my attention to the brunette who boarded the car at Queens Plaza.

"A two."

"No way," I argued on her behalf. "She's at least a two-point-five. Not quite a three star, but the possibilities are there."

Then the girl blew it by smiling at Mello first. Mello put his newspaper in front of his face to ice her. We laughed at her.

"Silly rabbit."

We got off at 53rd and Lexington Avenue. The plan was to start East Side, where we were more likely to rub elbows with the celebrity crowd or people who knew people, then work our way to the West Side for some fun.

Mello was eighteen but could pass for twenty-two. I, on the other hand, would have problems getting into clubs. But I wasn't concerned. I looked like I had a famous father. If they didn't buy that, I had fast talk like a grease-ball slider, a twenty, and a promise to drink club soda all night long. I was set.

The first place we tried had franchises in L.A. and London, and was a known hangout among young movie stars searching for someone to like them for being themselves. Limos pulled up and deposited guests at regular intervals. You didn't just show ID, pay, and walk in. You had to be selected at the door.

"Jackets required, sir."

"I been here lots of times," Carmello protested. "I never heard of this."

"I can assure you, it's jackets only, sir." The little guy's face was pale but immovable.

"We can't get in cuzza lousy jacket?"

"Those are the rules, sir."

I stepped in between them. "My friend here is allergic to layers of fabric on his arms. Makes him break out in a rash. Here's a doctor's note to prove it." I went into my wallet and pulled out a twenty.

Mello wasn't going for it and pushed my twenty back.

"I been here lots of times," Mello insisted. "I never heard this before."

The host smiled and said, "I think not. You, I would have remembered."

"Take that back." Mello had a handful of the host's shirt and throat. He waited for a retraction. The little guy's smooth skin blanched. His lips quivered and he started to sweat like he was going to pass out. He was not prepared to deal with anyone as dangerously unrefined as Mello, and just stood there appalled, offering his face to Mello's square fist.

It was now up to me to save everybody's face. Once Mello raised his fist he couldn't bring it down without delivering damage. Mello was always true to his word. Then there was the club host, who was determined to make Mello look as coarse as he perceived him, by refusing to fight back.

"Show some class, Mello. You hurt him, and there goes your probation. Let him go, man."

Slowly but not easily, Mello let the guy go. He punched the inner palm of his other hand with full impact. "Coulda been your face. Be lucky."

I had to get Mello away from there before he had regrets and wanted to go back. Mello didn't believe in threats. Threats were for big dogs with no teeth.

"Hey man, what's up with you?" I said. "We could have been in there. A little finesse. That guy *liked* you. We would have been in if you would have played it."

"Hey, that's not funny," he said, taking the guy's flirtation too seriously.

We walked until he cooled off. We were now in the lower forties, and I was missing out on all the celebrities.

"You should have worn a jacket," I told him.

"Don't start that jacket crap with me, man. I don't wear jackets. Too confining. You dancing with a chick and you start choking and sweating in all of those clothes—something you don't have to worry about," he cracked. Then he looked at me. "A bow tie? What are you supposed to be? Mr. Rogers and whatnot?"

"What's that suppose to be? Funny?" I shot back.

"While you're doing your wallflower act, GQing and contemplating that first move, I'll be dancing with girl after girl. If they not dancing with me they'll wish they could. Word."

"See, that's the difference between us, Mello. I'll be laying back checking out everything and *then* I'll make my move. I don't want every woman. Only the crème de la crème. Twenty-four carat gold. The Hope diamond."

Mello started laughing and said, "Only you could have a rap for not getting girls. Something we should know about you, man?"

"Yeah, man. It's quality, not quantity."

Now Mello was falling all over himself with laughter, and we moved on from our bad start.

"What's the plan, now that we blew your celebrity hang-out?" For a minute I gave Mello credit for his cunning. I wouldn't have been surprised if Mello had gone out of his way to blow it. He knew he couldn't converse in my league in a sophisticated atmosphere, so he blew it.

"Plan B," I said. "There's this other place on Fifty-eighth and First Avenue and—"

"Nah, nah. Just another jacket *GQ* joint. I say the Havana Club. It's the spot for chicks. And they be dressed like come and get it."

"You mean *mira, mira* land? Be serious . . ."

"No. *You* be serious. I want to have some fun, man," he practically whined, meaning he was getting fed up and could go into a mood swing on me.

I gave in. "Who are we going to see at the Havana Club?" We were doing a lot of walking and my suit was going to waste.

"See? Is that all you're worried about? Lots of stars hang there."

I shot Mello a "get real" glare. We compromised and headed toward this new club Mello was telling me about off 38th Street and Broadway. When we got there, people in small groups stood on the sidewalk waiting for it to be late enough to go inside the club. Music showered down onto the streets, and the club's floodlights gave the outside some excitement. Girls primped subtly, chatting and watching the watchers. There was a little bit of everything going on. A loose line had gathered across the street a few feet away. Couples took turns going in and out of the yellow cab that was parked opposite the club. For three minutes at a time they went in and came out. It didn't take a genius to know what that was about. I turned to engage in some mutual staring with two girls waiting to go inside the club, but Mello was headed for the "taxi line," so we kept moving in that direction.

Our turn came up on the line faster than I thought.

"Are you with it?" Mello asked.

Before I could hedge on my answer he said, "Let's take a hit."

"How do we know if it's any good?"

"I'll know." Mello jerked my arm with a look. There I was, following him to the backseat of the cab.

"Fifty for two."

My first thought was how totally stupid I look when I'm high. That I get paranoid and every other shadow becomes the feds. That I wasn't at home in my room lighting up a jay with Wendy or Cousin Randy. That anything, anything could happen. No one on 38th Street knew me, I had fake home phone numbers on me, and the only person who had my back was Mr. Destructocat himself, Mello.

"It don't look right," I told Mello. "This could be Ajax."

Mello ignored my baby stalling and went nose down to the glass, snorting sharply. This was my usual cue to pass on the stronger stuff and not give a damn for what was at stake, be it points or reputation. Instead, I followed Mello, eyes closed, nose down. We got out of the taxi and stood wordlessly on the sidewalk for a minute or two or ten. My heart fluttered briefly and my insides were coated with warmth, but that passed. The dark pulled down its shade and said, "Okay, D, it's on you."

We spoke briefly about the quality of the stuff, then lined up to get into the club. Mello went through, but I was asked to show ID. I flashed my temporary Princeton ID. The date of my birth appeared larger than the school name or my name, for that matter. I was betting the bouncer couldn't count backward. By now, Mello was already through the metal detector. No gun. Just a pocket knife to be picked up on his way out.

"No juveniles," said the bouncer.

"Juvenile? This isn't JV. This is clean living," said I.

He didn't even pretend to be interested and looked over my head to admit the next couple.

"Look. All I want is to dance a few dances. But hey. One phone call to my father and this place is closed," the coke made me say.

"So who's this father?"

I told him. He studied my face to catch me lying. I played the annoyed brat, giving him unrelenting deadpan until he recognized my "father" in my eyes.

He stamped an *M* for minor on my hand the size of marquee letters. Then he did the other hand. "If you so much as sniff a drink, you're outta here."

Mello gave me credit for getting in, knowing he would have left me hanging in a heartbeat. I wasn't worried. I knew I'd get in. While Mello went straight for a cluster of girls waiting to be asked to dance, I went upstairs to the balcony to get a better view. Why be afraid of heights? Up is a great place to be. You are above everyone. Above it all. Just hold onto the rail and everything is okay.

I watched Mello for a while. Then I looked for her. The girl that we would use for our contest. She couldn't be just any skirt. She had to be true contest for true knights. What kind of expressions did she make when you moved in close? Did she wait for you to point and spin her, or did she fight your direction? Was she dancing with you, or was she just dancing? Were her hands captive to the beat, or did she move her arms in a way so you couldn't help but take inventory of her bracelets, rings, and nails? Was she a dance, or was she the one?

Clearly, the night was young. *She* had not made her entrance. No use waiting for her. Time to circulate. I went down to the dance floor. Hmmm. There was a good place to start. Blondie, a Latina whose hair was dyed so yellow. Big nerve. Kinda interesting. Moved a little on the chill side—not like a desperate girl who is all over you praying you'll ask her for the next dance.

The dance ended. I watched how Blondie left her partner to sit out the next dance. I thought I'd let her regroup for a moment and prepare for me. I took my eyes off Blondie to check out Spandex Toe To Neck, who was getting loose in the center floor. Do girls really know what they be looking like? Spandex did. Bright red, from toe to neck. Leave Spandex alone. She looked too ready. I went back to Blondie, who was staring into space. Even better, Mello noticed Blondie. She was it. The big three star. I straightened my bow tie and let the music push me to Blondie. I extended my hand, palm up to conceal the *M*. Blondie held out her pinkie. They got class in the South Bronx, too.

I had to maneuver her to the center of the floor so we could star. Blondie had no problem being lead. She liked center floor, too. We started working out our signals, because we both sensed that we could flow together. She had a very nice touch.

KNOW WHAT I MEAN? KNOW WHAT I MEAN? I KNOW, I KNOW, KNOW WHAT I MEAN. Even the music was in on it. It boomed in the background, playing along with our silent dialogue. We smiled and danced like we knew, knew, knew. I hurled her so she spun in the center, where Mello could see her. You couldn't miss her! Blondie's hair knew the game plan and fell in all the right places. That was why she had dyed it like that. She knew how good we must have looked together and let me engineer her as I wanted.

Movement around us slowed down so the crowd could watch. Spin this, Mello.

He tried to look like he was into Black Party Dress, but I caught him studying us, trying to figure out how he was going to do it.

It was settled. This was going to be the game for the night. If he got her on the floor, two points. If she iced him, zero points. If she gave me her number, I was ahead. If she sat at the bar with him, he got the steal.

I was still putting the rules together, doing a samba with Blondie, when I noticed *her*. A girl. No. A lady. Sitting at a table telling a story to her friends. I had to know her name. She was in her late twenties. She made her group. I had to talk to her. Dance with her. Hear her sophisticated laughter in my ear. Some girls had windows for brains, and others you couldn't look through. She could keep me guessing forever—I had to leave Blondie and find out her name . . .

When I thought I was walking away from Blondie I found myself dancing alone. I wondered how long ago Blondie had left me. If Mello was watching me, how long was he watching me? Was I standing still or was I dancing? How do I get off the dance floor without looking stupid? Is this the bathroom?

When I did find a bathroom I lost track of time. I stayed in the stall for the rest of the evening. Someone banged on the door and woke me, and I came out. The crowd had thinned and the place was getting ready to close. I had to find Mello and get out of there before they shot us with the lights.

I spotted Mello and his date, already talking serious over by the coatroom. Then they disappeared.

I saw Blondie. She didn't look so bad in the light. She smiled at me, and we started talking. She was a bank teller. I was a sales trainee for an outdoor marketing firm. We exchanged phone numbers. I had the presence of mind to give her the fake number, thinking she was nice, but she would never do. Then I gave her cab fare, seeing that she had come alone and it was about three.

Mello came back without Black Party Dress.

"Let's go."

"Where's the girl?"

Carmello gestured *Does it matter?* I told Blondie that I'd call her, and then left her at the coat-check room. I had to leave her there. Mello had already seen me give her cab fare.

"What a chump, man. She got here by herself, didn't she?"

"As a matter of fact, she didn't," I bragged. "She came with someone but liked my style."

Carmello spat on that. "What you so happy about? You didn't even get five dollars' worth."

"Did you?"

"Asked you first."

"I got her number," I said, and felt obligated to add, "but I won't call."

"Yeah? Well I got *it*."

I knew I was supposed to be impressed by his easy conquest. And I was. But I liked messing with his mind. Carmello never knew how truly simple he was.

"Ten minutes in the coatroom? What did you really get? A handshake?"

"I got more than a stupid piece of paper with numbers."

"Well if I knew it was gonna be like that I would have tossed you a bag, man," I joked, but meant it.

"What for? She knew what she's doing."

"What if she's not clean, man? She was looking mighty professional to me."

"Hey, I'm not worried." Then Superman said to his side-kick, "To the trains."

"Sixth Avenue," I said.

"We're right here on Eighth. Thirty-fourth Street."

"No, not Eighth Avenue. It's nasty and full of bums, and I don't feel like rubbing elbows with your poppy, man."

Mello laughed at my off-the-wall crack and came back with, "My poppy and your mommy."

"That ain't funny, man, and I'm not going on the Eighth Avenue subway." I was hot, cold, sick, and thirsty. Gravity kept pulling down on my bowels. If I smelled piss I was going to lose it. I didn't want to go down Eighth Avenue, but there I was, following Mello down, down, down.

"You paranoid, D-Man. You need something for the edge."

Was I paranoid? No. Yes. I was sick and paranoid.

"We could get some in the station," Mello said.

"I don't think so. I don't feel right behind that first hit," I said.

"Then why'd you take it?" he asked like I was stupid in the first place. Now what was I supposed to say? Nothing.

"You goddamn punk," Mello said. "Shoulda said you wasn't with it."

"Shaddup, man. Let's walk."

We went down into the 33rd Street entrance to the subway station. There, much to my horror, was a line of bums waiting for us. I stuck my hands in my pockets and hunched my shoulders as though this would keep them from touching me. But they were so close. The bums didn't seem to bother Mello. He even kicked one in the shoe. "Wake up. It's your son."

The tunnel opened up into light and space. Then we walked over to this guy who was selling papers—the first sign of civilization. I was safe again.

Mello got a little agitated while I pored over newspapers. I figured it was because he couldn't read. I thought I'd play on it. After all, he messed with me and my bow tie. Insisted that we rub elbows with bums and walk through piss. Yeah. I picked up the *Wall Street Journal*. Not one photo. Just long blocks of text. Words on top of words, figures, graphs, more words. Very little breath or space. Yeah, revenge. Sometimes you had to break the code.

"Get the *Post*," he urged, turned off by the dull print. He hunched over, pacing back and forth as if the letters from the headlines could reach up and beat him into a nobody.

The humming of the train sounded. Mello had spent his last dollar and was going to jump the turnstile. The token booth clerk seemed otherwise occupied. Mello hopped over the turnstile, and I followed him.

"Pay the fare," chased us through a bullhorn from the token booth. We ran down the stairs to the platform, laughing like jackals. The train was there, but the doors were preparing to close. Mello jumped in between the doors and applied muscle. His head was pressed against the door. A pair of uniformed cops came running down the stairs. Looked like one was going for his revolver. Why didn't I see them coming before I jumped over the turnstile?

My gray linen pants were seconds short of being peed on. I was getting ready for whatever it took to not die. To be perfectly still so they didn't mistake my breathing for me going for my gun and shoot me in self-defense—as it would be told to the press. I could see it now: VALEDICTORIAN SHOT IN SUBWAY.

The door eased open and Mello grabbed me by the jacket, tearing my pocket, and pulled me into the car. The cops were on the platform, trying to signal the conductor to open up. The train pushed on. Mello banged on the door and beat his chest like King Kong taunting the cops.

I looked at my suit. "Hey, man, you tore my jacket."

WHEN WORLDS COLLIDE

I HAD absolutely no interest in the *Wall Street Journal*. I just wanted to cut Mello out and leave him staring at career-training posters. He got the message and had nodded out by the second stop. Seeing that Mello was snoring and I couldn't read with the train jerking, I folded the paper and closed my eyes. We must have been completely out of it because I didn't wake up until we passed Mello's stop.

Mello definitely was no stranger to sleeping on the train. He was comfortably slouched in the corner seat, blowing hard Zs. Since he had spent all of his money he would now have to think about where he'd sleep and eat for the next couple of days. Tonight he'd probably ride to both ends of the line until daybreak. I shook him hard when we reached the last stop. He opened his eyes, looked around, and said, "Aw, man. Shoulda woke me."

"So what," I said, trying to be cool about it. "You can lay over at my crib."

He stretched and said, "Naw. That's all right. I'll ride back."

Sure, partner. To the World Trade Center and back to Archer Avenue twelve times on the E train. "What's wrong? Too good to sleep at my house? You think we don't have sheets or something?"

"No, man. It's not that," he said. "I just don't fit in where worlds collide."

"What's that supposed to mean?" I looked dumb, knowing exactly what it meant, and that Mello was never big on explanations, and wasn't about to change at four in the morning. "Look. The bus is right there. We'll be home in five minutes. We'll crash and you'll be up and gone before anyone knows you were there."

We took the Q84 and went to my house. I knew the folks wouldn't like my bringing home a stranger, but they would at least be civilized about it. I hoped Vernon would still be sleeping when Mello left. Lydia, of course, would go out of her way to be annoyingly polite to one of my "little friends." Nana Dee, if she was up, would have sense enough to make him breakfast and ask him no questions. Kerri wouldn't notice Mello because he didn't look like someone who thought in BASIC, let alone knew what it was.

The porch light was on. Once I put the key in the door and brushed my feet on the mat everything changed. The bravado that made me tell lies, jump the turnstile, and invite Mello home wore off completely when I stepped on the carpet runners. We weren't two wild boys raising hell in the city. We were entering my parents' home.

Mello stepped over the mat and came tramping through my living room without any clue as to what he was stepping on.

The portrait of my great-grandparents caught his eye. So did Lydia and Vernon's wedding picture, the trophy case, and bean-head pictures of me in kindergarten. He picked up my father's hand-carved Zulu warrior, not knowing that there were things you just didn't touch.

His expressionless but too observant eyes gave me the feeling he was casing the house. Then I wondered if Mello would steal from me. No question. We always stole from each other then compared each other's moves. How would he know the difference between a few meaningless girls, High Man bragging rights, and, say, the family silverware?

It was too late to do anything and too awkward to say something. I had invited him to spend the night in my house— the guy who had said, "A skirt's a skirt. Your mother and your sister."

I showed him to the guest room and set the alarm for seventhirty. I wouldn't sleep. I'd keep my eye on him. "The family gets up at eight for church." I didn't have to say the rest.

My plan to stay up all night fell apart the moment I sat on my bed.

I awoke inside an office. It had to be mine. On the desk was a two-sided brass nameplate with Dinizulu on one side and Denzel on the other. The reflection in the paperweight made my nose broader and my forehead higher. I saw specs of gray in my hair, and I had a small goatee. I got it. I was my father.

Messages were thrown through the intercom. *Straighten up. Stay in line. Smile.* Everytime I did those things my head swelled with pain, especially when I smiled.

My office turned into a train station. The train was coming. There were new routes in front of me and shoulda routes behind me. I stood in the center where new routes met shoulda routes, not knowing where to go.

The train was s-l-o-w moving. I crouched and prepared to

jump aboard. When I looked around I was already in the car looking for a seat. Mello said he would trade seats with me if I had a seat for him. I said no way did I want his seat. He said look around you. Wise up. This is the only seat for you. I looked around. His was the only seat for me.

I looked through the window. Wendy was on a train on the opposite track. It wouldn't slow down. She wouldn't let me ride with her. I told her la-la means I'm sorry. She said I still couldn't ride with her. My train was too slow. I said I'll get off the slow one. She said you can't get off IT.

I wished she hadn't said that.

IT rose up and was coming at me. Orange and black paws. Head of a monkey gargoyle. ITs laughter was chilling.

"Denzel, come to the front of the class. Take off your face. Show the class your face. Denzel, we're waiting. Take off your face. Denzel . . . Denzel . . ."

I was trying to hit IT with the two-sided nameplate, but I couldn't figure out which side to use—Denzel? Dinizulu? Denzel . . .

"Denzel. Denzel."

I was being pushed into the seat facedown. ITs claws dug into my arm and I felt my warm blood dripping down my arm. I was trying to hide my face from IT. IT wanted my face.

I woke up with my face pressed into the pillow. IT was shaking my arm. ITs orange and black paws dissolved into my mother's hands.

"Son, who is that in the bathroom?"

I rolled over suddenly. I looked at the woman, Lydia, Mom. I couldn't see through her. She didn't turn into anything. She wasn't riding on a train. But her nails were going into my arm, and her eyes were mother serious. I smiled at her and she didn't know what to make of me. She asked again, firmly, "Who is that in the bathroom?"

129

"That's Mello," I finally said. "Carmello from work." Her face showed she wanted more. "Remember? I told you I was going out with someone from work. We fell asleep on the train and he missed his stop. It was late," I explained, and yawned in her face. She wrinkled her face and fluttered her eyes. I guess my breath was kind of tough.

"I had a good look at this Carmello," she reported, raising her eyebrow. The judgmental one.

What could she possibly know from a quick sideways glance? Half asleep and not wanting to start anything, I nodded. It wasn't even eight o'clock. I was frankly relieved to find myself in my room on Adelaide Avenue, not having to trade places with Mello on a slow-moving train.

"We'll be out before eight."

"What's this we? This is Sunday. A family day. *We,* as in your *fam-i-lee,* would like to see more of *you* before you go to *school.*"

I was thinking how utterly corny Lydia was when it dawned on me: Time was running out, and I had to tell them I wasn't going to Princeton.

"Now. Start getting this Mello together so you can show him out." Jeeez. My mother could say "Bad Area Bob" and make it sound like Wilfred Thornton Yates III.

Mello was still in the bathroom. I looked the guest room over, noting it was virtually undisturbed. He came out of the bathroom and was dressed.

"Sleep okay?" I asked.

He shrugged. In other words, don't make a big deal of it. Don't expect him to fall all over himself with gratitude.

"My moms is in the kitchen. We'll go in, say hello, and that will be that," I said to Mello. He got the picture and appeared to be straightening up his manner as much as he could. I introduced them.

130

"Nice to meet you, Mrs. Watson, or can I call you Lydia?" Before she could express her indignation he shot out, "No pancakes or eggs for me. I'll just have my coffee black."

He stopped Lydia right where she stood with her hand on the stove knob. His smile was wide and guileless so she knew he was joking. She shook her head and smiled back. She invited him to sit and have a little breakfast, but he insisted on just coffee. I wanted him out. The last thing I needed was Lydia getting all into his life story, then drawing conclusions as to what I was up to.

Kerri heard our voices and came running into the kitchen. Her face was unwashed and she was still in her robe. He was the first and only person she saw. He sat relaxed in Vernon's chair, with his legs extended to the side instead of underneath the table, as we had been taught to do.

"Hello, little one."

Kerri, like Lydia, allowed Mello to stop her cold and make her speechless. Mello turned to me and said, "You never said your sister was so cute."

Kerri blushed, managing a sheepish hello.

"Get dressed," I ordered her.

She spun around, tripping over her fuzzy slippers, and left the kitchen ever so grateful that I had given her someplace to rush off to, away from the guy who smiled at her unwashed face and uncombed hair and called her cute.

Great. A handful of words, a grin, and Kerri was a boy-drooling female.

By this time, Lydia had set a plate with two eggs, sausages, toast, and a cup of coffee in front of Mello despite his protests. My plate followed.

"I have to invite you to breakfast more often. It's usually go-for-what-you-know around here," I said.

Without fail, Lydia's mouth was wound up and running.

"Something wrong with your hands? If you want hot breakfast every morning there's the stove. Get used to it. I won't be running to Princeton to fry eggs. And if you think a college gal will drop her books to make you a meal I have news for you. This is a new day."

Turn it off, Lydia.

Mello looked at me. *You didn't tell her?*

No. I couldn't.

You wimp. You simp. You chump. All of this transpired in a glance, some chewing, and a crumpled napkin.

"So, Carmello, what college will you be attending?" my mother asked. It never occurred to her that I would have a friend who wasn't college bound.

"None," he said with no pain. "College isn't for me," he added, looking directly at me.

"What will you do?" Lydia practically gasped, because in her mind he just said he had a terminal disease. "A higher education is necessary in the world today."

"I'm going into construction with my old man."

"Oh. I see." *Then what do you want with my son? What could you possibly have in common?*

Son, I'll deal with you later on this. The "choose your friends wisely" speech was brewing in her eyes.

"Don't knock it," I said, feeling obliged to counter for my friend. "There's a lot of money in construction."

"Why break your back when you can use your brain?" Lydia backhanded.

"I love to work outdoors with my shirt open, Lydia," he said, while his tongue pushed around a mouthful of food so as not to be offensive. "I'm not a brain like Denzel, here. I don't want to sit at a desk or nothing like that to prove that I'm a worthy human being. It ain't necessary. I like to work with my hands. I do good work with these hands." The very things he would say while in between some girl's legs he said to my mother. Being nobody's fool, Lydia was at a loss for words.

I had stuck up for him, and he repaid me by stealing the words from my mother's mouth and sending my sister into hiding with her arms hugged around herself. And that tired lie about having an old man in construction. Puh-lease. Mello would step on his father if he saw him.

Seeing that he had finished his food, I said, "Mello. It's about that time."

Mello shoveled in the last forkful of egg. He let the yolk run down his lip and chased it with his tongue. My mother turned her back on him and said, "At least you have a sense of direction. So many young people are lost these days." My mother *never* turned her back when she spoke. Never. She looked like she was in hiding, poking overcooked food.

My father entered the kitchen and was clearly not pleased that his chair was being used. Mello stood up and there seemed to be no room for the two men to stand. They acknowledged each other after a clumsy introduction—clumsy because I didn't know Mello's last name. Or Bad Area Bob's, Shawanda's, Mikie's, the names of the two new guys in the crew, or that of anyone else connected with the job, except for Lizzie Chiu, but who was she? Jack was just Jack. Weber could have been a first name or last. Even I was using my name as an alias. It was my second summer hustling Miss Minerva's Assorted Cookies and World Famous Nutty Crunch, and I didn't know whom I was with.

We excused ourselves, and I walked him to the gate.

"Construction, man, what's that supposed to be?" I asked, hoping to put Mello on the spot. He didn't bite and came at me hard with, "What did you want me to say? I did six months in Rikers and I may do six more? Get real. That construction BS was for you," he said, throwing up his hands, through with the whole pretense. He looked up at the sky, searching for the right words, and then thought, to hell with it. "I told you. I don't fit in where worlds collide. You know how that is."

"No," I said, too angry to care how hard it was for him to find the right words. "Tell me about it."

"At least I didn't lie to my folks."

"What's that supposed to mean?" As if I didn't know.

"You didn't tell them you're not going to college. You let them think you're going. Everything cool. Everything's ivory leaf. At least tell them what's up. I mean, are you a man or a bow tie? Instead of frontin' this and pretending that, tell them. Tell them it's not you. Hey, look at me. I may be hard. I may be dishonest, but I don't lie about it. You, man? You false. Too false for everyday living."

"I didn't lie," I said, practically begging him to understand. The last thing I wanted was for Mello to see me coming up short. "I just didn't talk to them yet. I will," I promised.

"Hey. It ain't nothin' to me," he said, walking away carefree after he had mixed everything up. He reached up and slapped a piece of air that was supposed to be my hand in a high five.

Mello was an easy guy to hate. At that moment the hate ran deep. My partner. My cohort. My friend. Walked in my house and upset everything. Called my mother Lydia. Sat in my father's chair. And then called me false.

I just stood there for a minute and let everything drain out of me. I was steamed. When I came back inside they were all staring at me. Nana Dee must have been "filled in" because she was among the starers, shaking her head like a funeral mourner. Finally, Lydia said, "Son, your father needs help in the yard today. I'll drive myself to church."

"Yes, ma'am," I answered, knowing immediately it was as bad as it seemed. There was a lot to be said. And when it got said it would be ugly. Ugly enough for Nana Dee to keep quiet. Bad enough for Kerri to keep her eyes on her toast. Serious enough for Lydia to let me miss church.

I excused myself to change into clothing suitable for punishment. Dad had something in mind the equivalent of a beating. Something so humiliating he wouldn't allow the women in the house to see it. Strangely enough, I was relieved it was coming. I wasn't afraid at all—a remarkable revelation for someone who had made a practice out of avoiding pain. I didn't feel like talking my way out of it, fast, slow, or otherwise. I just wanted to get it over with. My head was filled with steam. I needed a beating to let it out.

Just how much did they see in Mello? Drug-coated eyes? Making girls into mommies? His prison record? His bullet wound? His scratch marks? His easy trade on life—any life? His earring? Or just his laid-back slouch in chairs that weren't meant for slouching?

When I came out into the yard wearing dungarees, Vernon and Mr. Randall were engaged in old man talk about what the sun promised. Oh, how they hated to get under it, "but there's no use running from the sun" were Randall's last words as he and Morris walked to church.

"We let this go too long," Vernon said of the yard. Then he grunted at me to get the mower started. I pushed the mower up and down the lawn. I wanted to get this over with—not talk in circles about the yard when he meant me. The yard wasn't out of control. I was in his territory in no time, mowing carefully where the grass met the hedges. When I got to a place where Vernon was trimming hedges I waited for him to move. I should have known he was waiting for me.

"Son, we haven't been on you because we know you're having a fling," he said, raising his voice to be heard over the mower. Then Vernon shifted into the role of the hip and understanding parent. I responded with the good son gambit, listening while mowing the lawn. "Just be mindful of who you're hanging out with."

I cut right to it. "In other words, you don't dig Carmello."

"No, I don't." His reply was impassive. "That's not the point."

I couldn't accept his tolerance because I wanted it to be out and he was doing what they'd been doing all along—giving me room for excuses, room for justification. Making it all right when they should have been raising hell.

I turned off the mower so he could hear me. Beat me if necessary. "See, Dad, you're being a hypocrite. You always say we're too hung up on classism and that we should relate to our people simply because they're the folks. You always say that if they're oppressed and they have one drop of the blood, then they're the folks. Now you're saying be mindful: He's not from the Black side of the tracks, and you know what, Dad? That's hypocrisy."

"As I was saying," he blew out his minor irritation and clipped hedges. He remained calm in spite of my outburst as though it had no merit, so why bother. Now I was doubly burnt. "The point is, you're supposed to use your head. Even a jackass can see a snake coming and knows to step back, go the other way, or defend himself. Even a jackass doesn't wait to see what shade of black the snake is. A snake is a snake is a snake, jackass. That don't mean get a closer look. And that damn sure don't mean let it in your front door. And that was a snake that you let in this house. As sure as everyone saw it, but you, jackass," he said easily, not angrily, but easily, like he could get used to calling me that. Me, a son he couldn't wait to crown with an African name. "The point is," he resumed, still calm, still in control, "one day you'll be the man of this house or your own house. How will you protect everyone in it if you don't see the simplest of things?"

"Dad, you're talking in riddles."

All clipping ceased.

"You got a problem getting me, son? Let me rectify that. Wake up and look at what you're doing before you get into a mess you can't get out of. Show a little common sense."

I just stood there feeling stupid.

Are you a man or a bow tie? Neither was the proper response. I couldn't let reason prevail. I was too angry and Vernon was there.

"I am showing common sense. I decided I'm not going to Princeton."

"You're going." He was calm. So calm he didn't hear the words that I had been struggling with for weeks.

He was going to hear me.

"Why? So you can brag to the white people on your job that you can send a son to Princeton?"

Vernon had that look: Do I hit him now, or say my say, and then hit him? "Here it is. You either join the real world. Work full-time in a real job, start paying room and board. Or you go to Princeton. There are no other options. I won't throw you out. That's not what I'd do to a son of mine.

"But boy . . . Come into my yard, eat my food, and call me what? I'll promise you one thing . . ."

It happened faster than I heard the promise. I was looking up at a shaded figure from the dirt. I didn't see stars, but I could taste the dirt.

"Now, pick yourself up and finish this mowing," he said in

that same calm voice as though he hadn't caused that hurricane to strike me down. "Then get out that can of white paint
and touch up those rocks in your mother's garden. When you
finish up in my yard you can sit in my house and think about
what you're gonna do."

FAIR GAME

*I*T WAS too hot to sleep and I was burning. Inside and out.

Digital time moved too slowly if you watched, too fast if you blinked. All I could do was stare at my alarm clock, watch twos turn into threes, and put tomorrow in order: Bring in trash cans. Turn on sprinklers. Put clothes in cleaners. Crush Mello like a roach.

I must have stared long enough. Threes turned into sixes. 6:36. The house was in motion for Monday morning. I heard footsteps come to a halt at the base of the stairs. There was a lot of um'hm-ing and um'um-ing. Lydia and Nana Dee were discussing me, the stranger I let into the house, and that I must have been on drugs, telling Vernon I wasn't going to Princeton. "Umhm. Dey's connected," Nana Dee said. "Nowheres b'gits nowheres. Trouble spells trouble." "Um'm. I just don't know. I just don't know..." said a weary Lydia. Heavier footsteps descended the stairs. Vernon added grunts and threats to the mill of worried female talk. Kerri was soon up and the talk ceased. An hour or so passed before the house stopped moving and they were all gone.

I clicked on the TV. Every station said what I felt all night. Inside and out. Today was going to be a hot one. The start of a three-day heat wave. Experts on meteorology and human behavior warned anyone who would listen to stay indoors. Too many people breathing too little air. Violence would erupt. Murder would result. Heed the warnings. Stay indoors. Keep cool.

This was all useless advice. Cool wouldn't do me a bit of good going after Mello.

It wasn't cool when he threw my house into an uproar just for the sake of saying, "Hey, D. I squashed your house." It wasn't cool when he took the words out of my mother's mouth, called her Lydia, had my sister tripping all over herself, Nana not speaking to me . . . my own father calling me jackass.

It wasn't cool when he caused my house to fall apart, then walked, leaving me to deal with it.

There were some things you just didn't touch. Some titles you didn't go for. Some grounds you just didn't compete on, starting with home. This was a given that didn't need a code.

If things were reversed and he invited me to sleep on his floor, I'da just said, "Cool. Wake me up at seven," and lain on that hard floor while who knows what crawled all over me. I wouldn't have been in his mother's face calling her by her first name like I *knew* her. No. I'da just said hello and thanks for letting me stay over, then left.

But he couldn't do that. Couldn't just sleep, get up, and

leave in the morning. Had to bring the contest into my house. Had to make himself known to everyone and turn everything inside out. On top of that, he judged me. Told me *I* was false like he was a man and I was a bow tie.

Now it was my turn to go after his house. He was probably laughing, wondering what I could do to top his conquest. After all, I had everything to take, and he had nothing.

Mello was not an easy target. There was no prize in exposing his illiteracy because his ignorance was a given. He didn't have anything worth taking. He didn't have a house I could walk in and take over. I couldn't make his moms into nothing Mello himself hadn't said openly. Couldn't snap on his invisible pops because he'd beat me to that, too. He didn't have a little sister to leave with her mouth hanging wide. I couldn't snap on his legion of stray kids because he seemed indifferent to them and their mommies.

He was laughing and talking to Bad when I came up the stairs and entered the outer office. One guess as to what the joke was. They chilled when they saw me, and Bad got up to sit with Shawanda. Mello couldn't stop smiling. I could hear his mind rolling: *Hey, D. I squashed your house, man. Your house and your mother.*

I walked across the outer office like everything was all right, and stood by Mello. "What's up with the face, grinning like a donkey?" I asked. "Must have been some strong medicine."

"Dope? Me?" He tried innocence, but it didn't come off. "What I need with that? I'm in love."

"Need a cure? Bang her once," I said, not interested. "That'll kill it."

He was serious about his revelation. Serious enough to take offense and to inform me, "That's my son's mommy," which caught me off guard. Usually when Mello said he was in love, he meant he had spotted some girl and wouldn't rest until he dogged her through and through.

"Ymangila? Her?" I don't know which surprised me more—him spilling it like a girl, or that he was in love by choice with Ymangila. Before, he was under her spell. Couldn't stand her, but couldn't leave her alone. Now he wanted to be in love with her.

"She's the one," he confirmed happily. "I'm seeing her after work. Got to tell her."

"Oh," I said carefully, knowing Mello had no idea how fast my mind revolved. "She don't know?"

"Naw, man. It just hit me like that." He snapped his finger and it came out sounding like a cracked walnut because his hands were so large. He was actually giddy and inched over to tell me all about it. "I went to see her after I left your place. We started really talking like we used to. Then I told her something deep. About me. Another girl would have stepped back. She didn't even blink," he said. "That's why she the one. The only one."

He dug into his pants pocket and produced a gold band with red stones. "My moms won't miss it," he said, polishing it on his shirt. He gave it to me to inspect and watched my face, afraid I wouldn't be impressed. When I said nothing he added, "I don't even think it's real. But it's all I got. Kinda looks like a wedding ring."

"No, not that?" I asked. "You're not taking a dive?"

"Like a kamikaze." He laughed until he was practically crying. "Why not? She sixteen, seventeen. Her pops will sign the papers. Her moms will cook us a dinner after we do it. I'll save enough money for us to move into our own place."

"Slow down," I said, returning the ring. "You already down and back from City Hall and she don't even know.

What if she turns you down? No offense, but Ymangila's no easy sell."

"So," he replied. "I say tomorrow, she say next week. That's so she can get her a dress and call her girlfriends. We fight about it. I tell her two days or forget it. She hang up on me, think twice, then send her sisters to tell me what time to pick her up."

"Just like that."

"Hey, I'm in her blood. She in mines. She wouldn't give me these," he bragged, slapping the arm that had those scratches, "if she didn't mean business. 'Sides, who she gonna get better than me?" I said nothing, which he took to mean agreement.

"So what's got you on this track?"

"Wanna know? Wanna really know?" He hesitated because he knew he was about to expose himself. But he was in love. His eyes were twinkling and he was amazed by what love felt like, and wanted to talk about it. "Seeing myself with Ymangila in a house that's got everything. A big living room with a big family picture. A kitchen where Gila makes eggs and sausage on Sunday morning. All of my son's things out on display—'cause he's gonna be serious. You'll see, man. Having the life. Stuff like dat," he said, grinning like he *could* have the life. My life. When he sensed that deep inside I was laughing at him because I had it like that and he never would, he got defensive, and said, "I gotta move on. I gotta be on my way somewhere. Either I'm in the world or I'm pulling it down. I might as well be on top of it."

I shook my head because Mello didn't have the tools to be on top. He didn't have the choices. I said, "It's your funeral. Do what you wanna do."

"Who's dying?" he said, undaunted. "If things go right this may be my last week gigging."

I questioned it. He started telling me about this contractor who was looking for guys to knock down walls and haul rubbish. That the guy promised him a job if he showed up next Monday at eight o'clock sharp. "All you need is muscle. And I got it."

"Hauling garbage with my bare hands? That's what they have tractors and pack mules for," I said, going too far, but what the hell. I had reached the point of not caring. "Couldn't be me."

"Pays ten times what we hustling here. I rather do that than hustle fifty cents a sale. What am I gonna do with fifty cents? I need a place. I got things to do," he said.

"It's your funeral," I repeated.

He was resolved. He was going to give it all up and marry Ymangila.

Mello thought he was slick. His plan was to stick his flag on my house, claim victory, then quit before I could retaliate.

This meant I had to move today before things cooled down. He couldn't leave thinking he had the title.

To celebrate Mello's clean break, we declared Fair Game on each other's territories to see, as an end all, who was the greatest. Fair Game meant throwing out all rules, doing whatever it took to sell high. If the opportunity arose, we could trash each other's cases. Cut in and steal customers mid-pitch. We only played Fair Game on special occasions because, of all the games, it was the most cutthroat. Worry about saying sorry later—just sell. Then when the day was over, whoever sold low had to slave for the other for the remainder of the week.

My plan was formed. He fed me with ammunition, not knowing I was loading up. Before this, I would never have used his dumbness against him. Just like he had thrown out the code, so had I.

I kept an eye on him in between my pitches. He was less

144

than good game. All he wanted was enough money to buy Ymangila some flowers and to get his son a toy. He let his opportunities go by. So far, he had all female customers, and he didn't do his thing. He didn't accept invitations to come inside and try to charm his way into a five-dollar donation. Didn't try to win a girl's sympathy by begging for a glass of water. There was no sleight-of-hand fast stroke down his fly. Instead, he called them miss or ma'am, something he stole from me.

Then I started to laugh. He was trying to beat me using my style: a smooth pitch.

Fool. Don't you know you're not me? Just because you walked into my house doesn't mean you're king or that the game is over. We've only begun to rumble. You haven't mastered me. You have to think fast to talk fast.

Mello was floating on a cloud, but that was his problem, not mine. I'd show him absolutely no mercy. Capitalize on his moment of weakness. Didn't he capitalize on mine and think nothing of it?

He had already supplied me with what I needed, and the plan fell into place. It was so perfect. So fierce. So cold. It was a righteous end all, and I was looking forward to carrying it out. Seeing the outcome in his face.

I moved on to my next block, leaving him behind. Volume. Volume. I had to sell volume. I started fixing prices any way I could, starting with a one-for-the-price-of-two con game. It wasn't working so I took a few losses at first, selling lower than the actual price. I had to establish momentum, the steady pass of money. Momentum and heat were everything. If I lost either one, the whole plan would fall apart. The main thing was, I had a plan, an immediate objective: make a big profit.

It didn't take much to sell a case. Even on a day when all that people could think about was cold water, I still sold gooey candy and stale cookies. It was the heat. Heat was energy, and I was a kinetic yo-yo throwing it out, reeling it in. Everyone else stood still, letting the heat control their pace. I was conquering everything in my path. Revenge was a great motivator. Now, instead of being hot, I was ice inside. I didn't even drip sweat. I was so nice.

"Ma'am, I won't take more than one minute of your time," I told the hausfrau whose lunch I was disturbing. "I'm a representative of the Summer Action Program. We are involved in fund-raising to keep our operation afloat. I see you're reading the paper. Perhaps you caught last week's article about our funds being cut. All is not lost, though. With the help of concerned community members such as yourself we are coming closer to raising the necessary funds to keep the foundation running."

"I'm not really interested," she said, and tried to close the door, but I said quickly, "Ma'am, it doesn't take much interest. All we're asking for is a four-dollar donation. To show our appreciation of your generous offering we will give you your choice of World Famous Nutty Crunch or Miss Minerva's Assorted Cookies. We're a nonprofit organization, so anything you can contribute will be appreciated."

She took longer to succumb than I could afford. And that annoyed me. She knew she was buying. Why drag it out? As it was, Mello was gaining on me and I wanted to shut him out of his block entirely. She chose the cookies.

I took her five dollars, hoping she wouldn't want the dollar change. She didn't, and I successfully pulled off yet another sale of one box at the price of two and a half boxes.

I wouldn't see Weber for another thirty minutes. That was a half hour too long. I ran down the avenue and backtracked to Shawanda and Bad. Like I suspected, they had both sold three apiece and were on a love break, holding hands, their lips glued together. I exchanged my empty case for Shawanda's, and gave her twenty-six dollars for it.

"What 'choo up to?" she asked—like she really cared.

"Selling," I said, and ran back to my territory.

Mello had progressed but hadn't finished out his block. I had to hope he was selling at the true price. He could get away with jacking up the price to three dollars, but he didn't talk fast enough to go higher. I figured I still had him beat.

Now it was time to have some fun. I cut in front of him to his next house. This meant he would have to keep an eye on me to make sure he didn't try a house that I had already covered. I could either sell and be ahead, or sabotage his remaining houses by doing quick, lousy pitches. Either way, I had him beat. I assaulted three of his houses in a row. "Lady, ya wanna buy some candy?" This was good for a hysterical threat to call the cops.

Mello was watching me. "You're crazy, you know that?" he called to me, seeing what I was up to. He didn't know how crazy.

I went back to my side of the street but was cut down at the gate. The owner had been watching me, saw my case, and let her dog out in the yard. I glared at the small mutt. Nevertheless, she had sharp teeth and danced frantically at the gate, wanting a thigh pork chop. I moved on to the next house, angry that my odds had been lessened through no fault of my own. I didn't mind them saying no after hearing my pitch, but this dog wasn't even going to let me in her yard!

Mello gave up trying to figure out which houses were sabotaged and started a fresh block. He had no chance of beating me but continued to sell. The thought of him chumping himself to ask me for money for Ymangila's flowers entertained me. But I gave that up, choosing to stick to my original plan.

He was in love. I wasn't.

I worked my side of the street steadily, determined not to sell for anything less than four dollars. Not only would I have enough money for my plan, I would undeniably be High Man and win Fair Game, no contest. I'd be real cool about it. I'd call it off, just to flash my superiority and then not speak on it. Why? Because the plan was sweeter than Fair Game. Much better than having Mello work for me one lousy week.

Weber came by to move us into a new area. I begged him not to. The area had life. I was selling high. Get me in the car, cool me off, and I'll get too cold. He thought I was on drugs. But when I showed him the money from the two cases I had sold, it was, "Anything you want, kid," and he gave me another case.

I was raking it in tough. Hottest day of the year and I was unstoppable. "Yes, ma'am. For a very worthy cause . . ." I had to sell big. This was going to be the big finish. Take everyone who wasn't fast enough. "Yes, sir. It is tax deductible. Your label is your receipt . . ." People would believe anything if you looked the part. "Yes, miss. The telethon will be on cable . . ." I switched back to Mello's side of the street to slow him down a bit. Had to give him credit, though. He crossed and started working the end of my block, so now I had to keep an eye on him. I threw him a cuss, but I wasn't really concerned. This game was getting too easy anyway.

I snatched up the remaining two houses on his side, waved the money in the air, and called out, "Fair Game."

Next block. I moved back over to my side of the street and started talking fast. Too fast for the pigeons. They might as well just hand it over. "Sponsors receive two gifts for a ten-dollar contribution. A patron receives four gifts for a twenty-dollar donation." It was a lot harder to push, but nothing beat the thrill when I got that ten or twenty.

Now I had to find Bad and Shawanda to reload on supplies.

Much to my surprise, Bad had actually sold ten, whereas I needed ten to guarantee a big finish. "Yeah, I'll cut you some profit," I told Bad, who chose now to develop some smarts. "Just give me these three." I sold those as fast as I picked them up, and at a great profit.

It was still very hot when I quit for the day. I walked to the pickup spot and waited for everyone to catch up. This was a good opportunity to put my money in order before Weber showed.

Weber's sixty-four dollars went into my left pants pocket. Out of that money I would receive sixteen dollars, plus High Man bonus, along with the rest of the money I made through the week. One hundred dollars cleared from "foundation" donations went into my right pants pocket. This was money that would go to good use. I set aside a ten spot for Bad, and the change left over went into my wallet.

"How many?" Mello asked when he caught up.

"You know how many. Question is, can you top it?" I said.

"Naw, man. I guess I have to pay the price," he said, although I knew he had stashed his donations, figuring, why give it all to me? I didn't mind. I would have done the same thing.

As I had promised myself, I let him off the hook and didn't say another word about Fair Game, High Man, or winning. There would be plenty of opportunity to dog him. We rode back to the office in good spirits, all for different reasons.

When we got back to the office we hung out in the street waiting to get paid, sensing that tonight had the makings of a good summer night—the kind that makes you stay out until two, three o'clock in the morning, not doing anything but standing still, occasionally swaying. Mello started things by twisting the cap off a fire hydrant for some kids who thought he was indeed Superman. Water jetted from the spout in a straight arrow, hitting the kids playing nearby. Suddenly there was music. Some guys had been working hard to turn their car into a strip cruiser. They had already torn out the backseat of the car to put in a set of speakers. Now they were testing out the sound. Shawanda bought a shrimp-boat platter, and everyone started picking at it. She pretended to be annoyed, but why else have it out there smelling greasy and inviting? Two girls, definitely JV league, started a handball game nearby, trying to lose the ball close to where Mello and I stood silently.

If only you hadn't walked into my house, this would be a great summer night. We'd be messing over those two little girls, then moving on to other things.

Mello was staring down at the flowers he bought for Ymangila out of his donations. In his eyes it was a good night. Possibly great.

But he was wrong. It was my night. The moment had not arrived yet.

Dave's crew pulled in and fell out of the station wagon completely wilted. They brought back almost as many full cases as they had brought out to the field. When they finished carting in their boxes they all ran back outside, headed straight for the fire hydrant, and started playing with the kids in the water. Mello took off his shirt and joined in at the hydrant, standing in the direct spray of the water. Bad was threatening to douse Shawanda with a large paper cup. He'd make a lunge like he was stalking her. She was backing away, leaving a trail of shrimp and yelling, "You better not!" high-pitched and helpless, but was nonetheless transparent. He kept coming at her with the paper cup.

"Bad, you ain't no good!" she squealed when he did what she wanted, and got her soaking wet.

I kept my distance. I wasn't about to get wet. I liked it where I was. Where it was hot. I stood back against the brick wall and dug everyone caught up in the festivities. Then I saw her coming with her sisters, pushing her son in the umbrella stroller. I got off the wall and straightened up. I had been waiting so long.

Mello picked up his tee shirt from the street and started drying his face with it. He had his flowers and his ring in his pocket, and was heading toward Ymangila and her son. I was on his tail.

He walked real tall. Was probably in his mind a few inches taller than he stood. And I thought, *good*. I want to catch you standing there like that, with the sun shining on your muscles. Stand tall while you can, Superman, 'cause I got the serious K coming straight at you. I said I'd do it. I said I would bring you down with Kryptonite. I didn't lie.

I overtook Mello's last step and got in between them before Mello could tell her.

"A little something for you and the kid." I stuck the money, one hundred dollars in messy ones and fives, between her long, slender fingers. She spread the bills as though examining a card hand. Her mouth kind of hung in a question, while her son looked up at me from the stroller.

"What the f--- you doing?" Mello.

"What you should be about doing." Ymangila.

"Ain't nothing but a wedding present." Innocent.

Mello grabbed my shirt and slammed me into the wall. His eyes were an arrow of hate pointed in my eyes.

Bad tried to break away from Shawanda, but Shawanda held Bad back and said, "He's wrong. He's wrong. Stay out of it." Weber yelled down from the office window, "Hey! Break it up!" But that was the extent of his intervention.

Whatever I didn't feel when Mello punched me in the face went to the back of my head, which was being repeatedly slammed against the wall. The only reason I was still standing was that he hadn't finished beating me into the wall. I started to double over, and he caught me and pushed me up against the wall hard so I was straight, or as straight as he could make me. He pinned me long enough to shoot his hate in my face and let me drop.

Ymangila kept asking Mello, "What's dis wedding present? What did he mean by that?"

I felt something shaking me. I couldn't see, but I knew it was Ymangila. Her fingers were long and slender and very cold. Her nails were sticking me. She kept shaking me, asking, "What you mean by that?"

I could hear, but I couldn't see. I had no sensation around my eyes whatsoever. I was blinded. But I could hear the silence of the crowd looking on in suspense. It was as though they were all watching something, waiting for something to happen.

Then there was the sound of some metallic object ricocheting off a hard surface until it broke glass in its final path. The last thing I remember was a different silence. They were watching Mello fade in the direction of the broken pieces.

ANOTHER JUST-SO FABLE

*B*EFORE I blacked out Shawanda said, "Leave him." When I came to, I found they had done exactly that. Left me curled up in broken glass and dried piss.

I looked around. The street had been partied on, littered, and deserted. The water still ran from the fire hydrant, but in a diminishing stream. Instead of music, there was the distant echo of barking dogs. The kids playing in the water and the handball girls begging for attention were in their railroad-flat houses. Bad and Shawanda, gone. Ymangila, her son, her sisters, the hundred dollars, gone. Mello, faded. The office window was blacked out: Weber and Jack must have walked right by me, if not over me.

It was not completely dark, but I couldn't tell time. My watch had shattered when I fell. I couldn't tell if I had been lying there for hours or minutes. Was I hurt or was I *hurt?*

My surroundings intimidated me. I felt small, even next to the fire hydrant. When I looked up from the sidewalk, the height and width of the railroad flats became distorted and unyielding as I searched over the two-story buildings for a piece of sky. I couldn't trust what filtered through my eyelashes since they were caked with blood. When I did see the sky, it was orange, blue, and purple.

The barking was no longer far away, but was closing in. The dogs must have smelled me and were coming to investigate. I had to get up. I laid my hands flat against the wall and pawed upward until I was on my feet. I fought off the strangeness in my head. If I gave into it I'd slump back down to the sidewalk. I took a few deep breaths and leaned my head against the wall. The brick wall cooled my head but could not remove the strangeness. Part of me found the impact of Mello's pounding fascinating. It was like being shot up with Novocain and checking out the effect because it seems so distant and funny. For instance, I was breathing through my mouth because I wasn't sure if I had a nose. My head was a hollow jar fit to contain ringing. As for touch, there were ten miles between the wall, my skin, and the feeling at the core of my hand. I was mummified.

Mello had beat the feeling out of my body and had tried to beat my brains out of my head. For that I was grateful. There was no way I could move, let alone walk, if all feeling descended on me at once. I wasn't standing straight, but I was standing and that had to be good enough to get me to the subway.

I was walking stronger by the time I made it home, but was far from being okay. The last thing I wanted was for my family to see me like this. I hesitated at the back door listening for sounds. No one was in the kitchen. I cracked the door open.

My sense of smell returned instantly because of the food that stank up the kitchen. Not that my mom's cooking stank. I just didn't want to smell anything as sharp as chili sauce. It made my nose bleed.

I nursed a weak hope that the smell of chili was the aftermath of dinner. It wasn't. When I opened the door wider and entered, I heard metal hitting plates. And there was also talk coming from the dining room, meaning there were at least two of them. It didn't matter which two were seated. Any two were the wrong two.

I couldn't turn around. They had already heard me. Now they were going to see me.

I tried to walk steady so it wouldn't look so bad.

They were all in the dining room finishing a meal of sloppy joes and corn on the cob when I walked in on their debate. This was typical Watson talk taken from headlines and then woven into hypothetical situations. Vernon, the instigator, would cast out statements, and Lydia would take the bait. Nana would dismiss it all as nonsense, but had to have her full say on why it was nonsense. Kerri and I were always amused by these family discussions, and chose to side with the parent we most needed as an ally at the time.

In spite of my attempts to walk steady, I set off a land mine in their eyes. My mother dropped her fork. My father intercepted: Don't you dare run to him.

"Evening, Son." He was especially pleasant, but his message was clear. I had made my choice; now I had to stand by it. "Nice of you to make it for dinner."

At the moment I had trouble speaking because I hadn't used my mouth, not even to spit since Mello had hit me.

"Vernon, he's—"

"Good evening, sir. Ma'am," I said, finding my tongue, lips, and teeth in a hurry. I still had teeth. All of them, I thought, sliding my tongue around my gums. "If you'll excuse me, I have to wash up."

"You do that," Dad said, and continued the discussion. The topic was Afro-American commitment to South Africa.

I hobbled through the room with their eyes on the back of my head and my stiff movement. As I rounded the dining table and turned toward the stairs, I heard my mother gasp, her chair scoot, and my father's voice command like a dog trainer, "Sit." I heard Nana saying, "Now wait a minute," and Dad saying what he would never have said to his mother before: She could leave if she didn't like it. This was his house.

I stripped in the bathroom. I could only recall two blows to the face, yet I was bruised all over. My rib cage was scraped. My outer thigh was sore like it had been kicked. Maybe they had all taken turns on me after I had blacked out. The spot where my head hit the jagged wall had stopped bleeding. Streams of dried blood decorated my neck, clothing, and chest. I figured once I was cleaned up, it wouldn't look so bad.

I moved onto the hardest part—confronting myself in the mirror. It was worse than I had imagined. My face was completely swollen. My eyes were puffed slits. My lips, black inflated tubes. I had a nose, but did I want it? It looked broken and twice its normal size. And a Watson nose, too? I couldn't take it.

I stood in the warm shower, holding onto the towel rack, still feeling weak. I knew I had to get back in there, sit down, and show them I was all right. Show my father I was a man who wasn't about to cry so he could call me a jackass for fooling in places where I didn't belong. I may have *known* I didn't belong, but I wasn't about to say it.

I put on my pajamas and joined my family as fast as I was able to. They were having dessert. Nana's place was empty.

156

Although I wasn't hungry my mother put my dinner in front of me. My teeth were too loose for corn on the cob, and all I needed was sauce to sting my cut lip. I picked at a slice of bread.

My father hadn't stopped talking about the political unrest in South Africa and our responsibility to "our brothers." He then asked for my opinion. Would I put my degree on the line to protest America's lack of commitment to Black South Africans?

My immediate response was gratitude. Dad was letting me back in. I may have been a jackass, but I was still part of the family. I wanted to smile at him and give my usual antagonistic opinion so we could go at it like we used to.

My mother was outside of things. She didn't understand what was going on and was seething because Dad had forbidden her to mother me. My sister just sucked on her dessert spoon, staring at my swollen head. Even Kerri had *some* common sense and wasn't about to open her mouth.

"Dad, the way I see it—"

My mother stood up.

"What we *need* to do is take care of what we have right here instead of over there where our help is neither wanted nor appreciated." Her voice dug deep under the table and came out through the small but noticeable vibration of the plates. "We *need* to take care of what's underneath this here roof!"

Her indictment had nothing to do with South Africa. Kerri and I cleared the room. They were going to start.

Later that night, after everyone was asleep, my father woke me and took me to the hospital for stitches. I sat tight for the ride, waiting for Dad to spin another just-so fable about the snake and the jackass. Instead, he asked me again if I would put my degree on the line for a principle. I told him I wouldn't and gave my reasons.

That was my last day in the crew. Fat Jack never called my house to beg me to come back. I couldn't have cared less what they did with my pay or my High Man bonus.

Without the job to go to, or friends to hang out with, I had a lot of time to think. Everything passed before me, but I couldn't escape my thoughts about the quest for High Man.

I had made an art of achieving the most while expending the least. Mostly because I knew I could, and because I hadn't been challenged. But for High Man, twenty measly dollars, I had called on every resource available to me. As soon as I had won the title, my reign was over and I had to win it again, which meant I had never had it.

It wasn't for the money, but to beat Mello. Had to beat him more than I had to get paid. Sure enough, I'd beat him, and it would be great. I'd get happy, dance all over my High Man title like I had defeated the invincible giant, when in reality my competition was someone who could never truly step into my world, go places I could go, be who I could be.

Thoughts like these depressed me. I depressed me. I didn't want to be around anyone, and no one wanted any part of me either.

A few weeks ago it had seemed like I had so many options. Time had run out, and in reality I had only one.

My qualifications were nothing to start a career with, so a job was ruled out. I *could* get into another college, but I'd have to wait a semester to begin classes. I should have been hustling to get into another school instead of running around wasting time, and now it was too late.

This left Princeton, the only place where I would be expected and welcomed in the fall. I had no other choices that my family would accept. With some luck I could survive the first semester and transfer to a college closer to home. I knew I needed college. I didn't necessarily need four years of Princeton. As for my family, they would have to accept that I had at least tried when I came home after one semester.

When Kerri was out of the house, I went into her room and borrowed a few books. I read them from cover to cover, waiting for my swellings to go down. I had nothing better to do.

After the fourth book I gave up on reading. Couldn't get through a chapter that didn't, in some underhanded way, throw the quest for High Man in my face.

I tried confronting myself in the mirror. It took some psyching, but now I could stand to see my face. My head was returning to its normal size, although I was far from normal looking. Even when my family saw me, their faces showed repulsion, curiosity. They wanted to know what I could have possibly done to deserve getting my face battered in.

I could have come up with the kind of story that would have been acceptable to them and also save my rep. I just didn't feel like it. I was either very tired or feeling beyond all of that.

There was no clean explanation for why my head was swollen and my body was beaten, or why I had dragged the foulest-smelling street urine into my parents' house. But there was always the truth.

My father never asked me what had happened. He seemed to know without having been there. Not the details, but that the snake had bitten me. My mother asked from time to time how I was feeling, patting my shoulder, leaving an opening so I could run to her, but I never did, and she was sullen with the knowledge that I wouldn't. Nana stayed in her basement apartment, under a self-imposed exile, which was too bad because I was missing her.

The only person who said something was Kerri. "Did it have something to do with that gorgeous guy you brought home?"

Bam. On the mark. As her elder I felt obliged to ignore her.

"Did you try to steal his girl? Did you fight him? That was dumb. You can't fight *him* and 'spect to live."

"Kerri, leave me alone." One day she'd figure out I was no match for her either.

Did I try to fight him.

If she only knew how ridiculous and unlikely that was she would have asked me something else. A fight implies both offense and defense. There was nothing that I could have or should have done on my behalf. It was understood that Mello, in his blindness, could have killed me using barely any force. Instead, he held back, looked me in the eye, and let me drop. In a way that may have only made sense to us, I owed him my life.

What happened between Mello and me was inevitable. Why it happened made sense, but was not meant to be explained to the folks. Mello lived the code to the wire. He let it be known who he was and what he was about. A dude was always cool in Mello's book as long as he wasn't a punk. Make a move if you're bad enough. Just don't punk Mello. Cross that line and you had to be hurt. Well I had crossed it and Mello hadn't lied.

Eventually Kerri's smugness and the quiet concern of my mother and Nana drove me out of the house. I looked up Cousin Randy, only to find that he had already left for school. From his house I walked over to Andrew Jackson to look around, see who was there. I recognized a couple of cross-country runners on the track, preparing for the fall season.

I knew them. I could have gone on the field, BS'd around. I just didn't feel like it. I stood there on Francis Lewis Boulevard watching the runners, with my fingers hooked into the warm steel fence.

After completing a milestone, the runners saluted the mural of athletes and our motto painted on the field house: WE CAN BECAUSE WE KNOW WE CAN. Our cheer. Now it sounded as it looked. Painted big and white, like a lot of loud talk. Sounded real nice when a hundred voices shouted it together. But the truth was, some of us be shouting, knowing we could. Some of us thought we could. Some of us fronted it like we could, knowing it was a lie. The rest could have cared less.

I should have known. I used to lead the cheer; I was the proof. The absolute proof. I was valedictorian. I was class president. Was, was, wuz. Gone like vapor.

It was now time to walk. I couldn't stand in the same spot looking at something that was no longer relevant.

I left Andrew Jackson and walked away from the main boulevard. Looped around 198th Street, around Murdock so I wouldn't have to see the candy store. Over to Wendy's house. I had walked this route for four years. I'd probably never have any reason to come this way again. I just wanted to see Wendy. I didn't care if she saw me with stitches in my face. She could even know how I got them—and I imagined, when I told her, it wouldn't be news to her. I just wanted to say goodbye to Wendy before she went to Brown. Just good-bye.

When I got to Wendy's house, her mother opened the door before I reached for the buzzer.

"You're too late. Wendy left yesterday." Some things would never change, though. Mrs. Kilpatrick still managed to knock the gladiolus out of my hand.

"I'd like to write to her, but I don't have her address."

She asked me to come in. "What happened to you?" She stepped close, examining my face.

"I got beat," I told her. "I'm okay." I realized I sounded like Mello. Like it was no big deal. I could take a punch.

"Someone really ran over you," she said after going over every stitch on my face. "You look just awful."

It dawned on me how much alike Wendy and Mrs. Kilpatrick were. Bold. Not a pretense or apology in the world. Those were some of the things I liked most about Wendy. She wasn't hiding in her femininity.

"I thought you'd be gone by now," she said, looking for paper to write on. She took a pad from the coffee table and sat down on the sofa. I also sat down.

"Saturday," I said. "The folks are driving me up to school." Saturday was two days away, although in my mind I had put it off for another week.

"That's nice," she said, glancing up, then began writing. "We took Wendy yesterday. Her uncle and I. It's a beautiful campus, you know," she said with pride. She told me all about it, wanting to talk about her daughter. She also told me about Wendy taking a trip to Ireland and how Mr. Kilpatrick had always wanted Wendy to go there. I didn't even know that Wendy had left the country.

Mrs. Kilpatrick missed Wendy. She had already made a Wendy shrine in the living room, next to the shrine of her dead husband. Wendy's shrine consisted of diplomas, honor roll certificates, trophies, science fair ribbons. Mr. Kilpatrick's shrine displayed a police academy graduation photo, wedding picture, trophies, newspaper clippings. Graduating from childhood was like dying.

I was glad Mrs. Kilpatrick had let me into her house, but I was sorry Wendy wasn't there. Sorry I was nothing. Had no titles. Depressed that I was going to Princeton and that I had to start from nothing.

I took the address from Mrs. Kilpatrick and left.

My folks tried to get me interested in college. They got me a footlocker. Took me for some last-minute shopping. Started up again with the run-on lecture; keep your brain in your head, not in your tail. Don't get sucked into the party whirlwind. Be a leader, not a follower. Nana got me alone. "If that Princeton mess is too far away, you come on home." But I knew better than to hold onto that. Dad ruled the household. The only way Dad would accept me coming home prematurely was if I was thrown out for protesting the cancellation of Africana Studies 101.

Friday the house was very quiet. Like Wendy's house. All lively talk was banished. I was sure there would be a lot of family festivities and rituals. I was actually disappointed that there was no big feast with relatives and friends. Instead, they were eager to send me off. My mother tore through the things I set aside to take with me, and decided what was going and what was staying. In no time she threw my things in a wardrobe bag and footlocker. Together, standing in the vestibule, my luggage resembled a body and a coffin.

I stared up at my ceiling, knowing I should get some sleep. Dad had said we were leaving early in the morning to beat traffic. My stomach rumbled. Tomorrow was the day. The beginning of the end. How could I sleep knowing what was ahead of me? How could I sleep?

Finally I did.

Will the family of the accused rise.

Will the congregation rise.

Will the Summer Action Program rise up and step away.

Will the Princeton student body rise.

Look down upon him. Look down upon him. Denzel, remove your face so they can see you.

I was kneeling in a clearing between two white buildings with Grecian pillars. Tigers guarded me on both sides. One by one, the rows of people began to stand and look down on me as though I were dead. As they stood, their height became exaggerated and I seemed even lower to the ground.

My graduating class. The congregation. The crew from the SAP. The Princeton student body. My family.

I tried to look away, but my face was like a magnet and the people were the metal. My chin was being pried upward from my chest. I looked for a sharp stick, an object to fight with. If I could think about it, the stick would appear. My mother's voice said, "You can't have what you don't use." Kerri was jumping around like a puppy. "Ooooh! I'll use it! I'll use it! Can I have it?"

A monkey gargoyle shouted "Remove your face, Denzel. Let them see you for the last time."

One by one, each group leader shouted, "Remove your face, Denzel. Remove your face so we can see you." Mello led Ymangila, their son, and the crew. Kerri led my family. Wendy led a cluster of faceless girls. They kept coming.

As they made their rounds they walked away, intoning, "Leave him. Just leave him."

I tried to run after them. Tried to get them to come back . . . Come back . . . The tigers closed in on both sides of me. They raised their magnificent paws in unison. The monkey gargoyle chanted, "This is IT! This is IT!" and paws descended like fire on my flesh.

When I woke my family was gathered around me, trying to hold me down.

PRINCETON FOOTNOTES

W E ARRIVED on campus shortly after ten. At first glance, there was nothing awesome to make you bow down to Princeton. The campus in late summer seemed very ordinary. The only haunting thing about the grounds was the abundance of trees, which gave the feeling of being completely shrouded in leaves. To get the full effect of being at Princeton, you would have to venture deeper into the grounds.

Maybe had there been some ferocious structure at the school's entrance I would have been too impressed and too terrified to have taken the summer program for granted. Maybe not. All I knew was the time I had used for planning my moves had run out. The motion around me was going forward, and I was reluctantly getting blown in that direction.

My family was excited to be there, but for my sake they contained their excitement to a shallow glow of pride.

I tried telling them the night before that I didn't want to go to Princeton, but they refused to understand. My words made no sense. Whatever I did say got drowned while they chanted, "It's only a dream."

Now that we were there, the campus seemed to contradict my fears with its small-town demeanor. No sense trying to explain what my family couldn't comprehend or accept: Denzel, fear, and failure. They'd say that was a bad dream, too.

We got out of the car. The ground didn't open up and swallow my foot when I stood on it. Actually, nothing happened that could be interpreted as an omen. Except for the Princeton Jazz Ensemble playing "Hold That Tiger" in Prospect Gardens as we passed, my return to campus was uneventful.

My father, though, made a ceremony of us, the men, dragging the luggage. My mother, Nana, and Kerri walked behind, making note of everything. They were so excited and proud.

I was assigned to Mathey College and would be dorming in Campbell. Nana said I thought you was going to Princeton. I tried to explain that the school was divided into five colleges, and that I was in Mathey College. She insisted I was being gypped.

When we got to the dorm, one of the residence assistants handed me a folder of orientation activities and directed us to my room. After we got my things settled, we attended the family luncheon hosted by my college. Instead of enjoying the food and the entertainment, my parents counted Black faces—none of which I knew. My mother's eyes sent out coded messages as we passed these families. You're here, too? So are we. Glad to know you. I wished she'd cut it out.

When things began to wind down I hustled my family out of

the luncheon before they could form any coalitions. We went back to my room to see if my roommate had moved in. I was relieved to find that he hadn't. Not with my folks still there. They'd use any opportunity to thread my achievements into the introduction, or mention that we were from Addesleigh Park. They had no idea that these things became insignificant by virtue of my acceptance to Princeton.

"This bed is too small," my mother criticized.

" 'Sposed to be," Nana quipped. Sex. Nana was worried about sex when I was flooded with homesickness.

My father had gone through all of the Princeton literature that was lying around. "They have African Studies *and* Afro-American Studies," he informed me.

"Look," Mom exclaimed. "They have a branch of the NAACP. Affiliate yourself right away," she ordered. "We're members."

"Your mother's a member," Dad corrected. Dad had once spearheaded a petition to rename the Colored People.

Nana cut in between them. "Son. You leave all that mess alone and tend to your lessons, y'hear."

To get in on the act, Kerri wailed, "I want a tee shirt." Not that anyone paid her any mind.

That was when my roommate came in with his father and two brothers. Already drowning in orange and black Princeton wear, he bounded across the room and shook my hand, introducing himself as Niels Fenwick. Our families kept their distance and spoke cordially from across the room.

It was time. As annoying as they were, I didn't want my family to go. I walked them to the car, at a slower pace than when we first came. I could feel it. Someone was going to break. Maybe me. I was counting on Mom's reserve to keep us all from falling apart. She was the first to break down, crying that her baby was a man. Then Nana started telling me all about myself, saying how I was hell-bent on diving into wild college goings-on and misplacing God. "Just remember. You may lose Him, but He'll be watching." I yes ma'amed her and Nana broke, too. She was so used to me wisin' back at her. Humility wasn't what she expected or wanted. Kerri kissed me on the cheek and promised to take good care of my things. My father, who I was sure would shake my hand, hugged me instead. When everyone else was in the car, he asked me if everything was going to be all right, meaning did I want to switch roommates. I said everything was going to be fine.

They left me. I slipped my hands into my pockets and walked slowly back to the dorm. I pulled something out of my pocket. Someone—my mother, father, or Nana—had slipped a return bus ticket into my pocket. Good for ninety days. I was relieved someone had listened.

I spent some time with Niels and his family. As Niels had demonstrated, the Fenwicks were an exuberant clan. They insisted that I come with them to dinner, insisted that I tell them all about myself (and vice versa), and that I come home with Niels on a break.

Niels was from East Islip, way out on Long Island. He was full of that outdoor spirit, the picture of health. He wasn't especially tall, but was nonetheless an athlete, filled out and solid. He played field and ice hockey for fun, and was into Greco-Roman wrestling, although his heart was in rugby. He planned to choose architecture as a major, but was going to fill in his schedule with as many music courses as his schedule would allow for diversion.

"Princeton offers great courses in music from the Medieval period," he said, beaming. Niels loved Medieval everything. He was going to trace his family's tribe and castle one day. Would I dare tell him about my father's search for our roots? Maybe later, if I was still at Princeton.

When he inquired into my academic plans, I said I was undecided, which was the absolute truth. It wasn't until very recently that I had accepted coming to Princeton. Not that I had had a choice, nor was I dying to be there. I had spent the best part of my summer trying to force Princeton into a black hole. I sure as hell didn't see myself wearing an orange and black beanie or parading a tiger on my chest. I didn't doubt that while I was having nightmares, Niels dreamt of riding the tiger.

Niels dominated our conversation, outlining his five-year academic plan. His general enthusiasm for being on campus was too loud for me. I was still testing out the whole idea of being there, and quite frankly, I didn't want to get too used to it.

By the way he kept initiating things, I could tell Niels felt responsible for me, thinking I was this quiet dude. Quiet and lost. Waiting for direction. Ordinarily I would have set things straight and put Niels in his place, but I was out of it. No juice. No spark. No score card. Had to be ill. There I stood, sabre to sabre with a worthy opponent, and I could have cared less. Not even to make those point-for-point comparisons that made the game worth playing. The game was null and void. We had so little in common. Niels was that uniquely well-rounded student that the admissions guide described. I, on the other hand, began to feel obtuse next to Niels, but at the same time, I did not want to be him. Niels was just too gung ho.

"Have any plans for tonight?" Niels asked after his family had left. "The Princeton Footnotes are having an open house."

The Footnotes were a men's singing club, of which there were at least a dozen. Niels wanted to check out each one. He was in Princeton heaven.

"C'mon. Grab your jacket," he said.

He was so sincere it wasn't worth the loaded shot.

We went. It was corny. Niels dug it.

He was all right. He was going to take some getting used to. Niels was a slob. A complete slob. Sure, he'd try to hide it. Make the ultimate sacrifice. Hang up a jacket. Use the trash can. Make his bed. I was certain it was all for my benefit. It didn't last too long. Niels reverted back to his true sloppy self. He quickly forgot about those hospital corners and just threw the covers over the untucked sheets. I couldn't bear to look at it, let alone have it in my room, so I'd end up making his bed.

I always knew I was neat, but I had no idea how neat until those first few days with Niels. I was born into neatness. Everyone at home was neat. I never knew any other way to be.

Overall, he was okay. We worked out a stereo, lights, and visitation schedule, which was a must because Niels was outgoing and hospitable, attracting people wherever he went. When we went to the dining hall, he'd park his tray at the jock table and expect me to sit with him. It didn't matter that they were future congressmen, doctors, or engineers. They were jocks first and foremost with stoogelike mentalities, and Niels was always in the vortex of their food fights. Niels fit in with them. His dream was to move into Blair Arch Tower when he made the rugby team in his junior year.

We were always on the go. There wasn't a social activity that he could resist, and I just went along. Niels reminded me of someone who had never been away from home and was going berserk. I knew I should have been more excited about being on my own, but I wasn't. For one thing I was worried about classes. Being found out. Being sent home.

Niels had no worries, just a lot of energy. He wore me out, having to check out this and that. Our second night we went on a hunt for gargoyles and tigers all throughout campus. The following night we attended mixers and open houses hosted by intramural teams. I knew my folks wouldn't be thrilled with the sight of me following Niels around. But it was either that or sit in my room and imagine what classes would be like.

After a week's worth of orientation activities with Niels, I was resolved to my orange and black reality. I wasn't going to use that bus ticket someone had slipped into my pocket no time soon. I was here. At Princeton. Just another small point in an orange and black world. I was somewhere on the very bottom. If I got to see the toes of the smart folks, then I was surviving. I didn't have to worry about making plans to transfer closer to home. Once my folks saw the straight Cs that I would be happy to get, they'd have me taking correspondence courses from the safety of my room—with one of those "accredited" universities found on the back of matchbook covers.

I fell into bed the night before classes, and kept my prayers simple. "Walk me through the nightmare. Amen."

HONOR STATEMENT

NANA was right. There is something to be said for the power of prayer. My bed turned out to be a pretty safe place. For the first time in months I slept incredibly well. I would have slept longer except Niels woke me at seven-thirty.

"Get up. Let's go have breakfast."

"You go have breakfast. My class isn't until ten o'clock," I complained. My bed was warm and I was having a good dream.

Niels laughed at me like *I* had to be joking. "Will you get up? I'm hungry," he said in that gosh darn country boy way of his.

"Then go eat. Leave me alone."

Niels tore the covers from my body.

I threw my pillow in his face. "Die, cretin."

"C'mon, c'mon," he said, throwing back the pillow. "Let's get a move on."

Niels was a creature of habit. Had to eat three meals daily, at the same time. Couldn't eat without laughter and high jinks going on around him. This wasn't too hard to figure out. As much as Niels loved being at Princeton, he was fighting off homesickness and loneliness. If Niels ate one meal alone, or had two seconds of silence to himself, his roof would cave in and he would realize he was on his own.

He waited for me to shower and dress, then we went to the dining hall. I sat down to eat my cereal, while Niels sat opposite me with his plate heaped face-high in food.

"So, did you call her?" he asked with his mouth full of bacon and home fries.

"Hey, man, close your mouth when you chew. It's called table manners."

Niels laughed, shoveled in a double helping, and asked again, "So, did you call her?"

I gave up. He was just trying to irk me because he knew I was half awake. "Call who?" I asked.

"Wendy," he said. "Didn't you see the message?"

I stood up. "Message? Wendy? She called me?"

"If you're going to behave like that every time a girl—"

I pushed his plate to his extreme left. "Where's the message? What did she say? Did she sound angry?"

Niels reached for his plate but couldn't get it. "All she said was to tell Denzel his friend Wendy called and to call back. Now give back the plate."

"She said 'friend'?"

"Watson. Get a grip. People are staring," Niels said.

I ran back to the room. Wendy's message was on the chair underneath Niels's sweater. I picked up the phone and started dialing. My heart was jumping. The cereal wasn't helping my stomach either. I was thinking of an opening line when she said, "Hello." I was so glad to hear her voice that I blew my lines and blurted out, "Wendy! You sound so good."

"You don't. You sound out of breath," she said. "Cut it out, will ya? I'm not a ghost."

"I'm so glad you called me," I confessed. "I was gonna write you. I even started the letter. I'd read it out loud, but it's not that kind of letter."

"You can send it," she said, which was merciful on her part. No matter how sorry I was about things, I just couldn't say it over the phone, and the letter dripped sap.

There wasn't much time to talk because she had a nine-fifteen class. We had to fit us, and the tail end of a summer, into forty minutes. I told her about Mello and Ymangila. Talking about them made them seem so distant. And they were. They had nothing to do with what I was about, and I had no place in their lives. When I told Wendy how Mello and I had parted, she said it served me right. I laughed. As always, she spoke the truth.

I couldn't believe we were talking. Wendy had had a great summer. She told me about her trip to Ireland. She met a guy there. Called him every day when she got home. Her mother would flip when the bill came.

We made plans to hang out during the holidays and visit each other's schools, although I got the feeling she was fitting me in. Her voice told me I was just one of the boys. It was hard to believe or accept, but Wendy had a life that didn't involve me. I had thought about her all summer. Yet after the blowup at her house, she didn't think about me twice, not even in anger. It was too bad because at this point I would have given her anything.

"Dog, Wendy. The least you could have done was send me a postcard."

She just laughed. We both laughed. She said she had to go. She had class. We said good-bye.

I rolled around thoughts of Wendy until I entered my first class—economics.

I was relieved to find myself in a huge lecture hall surrounded by students. All I had to do was listen and take notes. I wouldn't have to worry until Wednesday, which was when the lecture broke up into smaller classes and my professor could actually see me, and, even worse, expect me to speak.

Once the lecture began I listened intently and wrote furiously, keeping my eyes down and my mouth shut. Even if I thought I knew something or had a question, I kept it to myself. My aim was to maintain a low profile for the whole semester. The last thing I wanted was to call unnecessary attention to my ineptness so that I'd be squashed unceremoniously before my classmates. Can you imagine the echo of two hundred hyenas bouncing off the walls of this cavern? It would never die down.

As the week went on, I found none of my classes to be how I had imagined. Compared to the intensity of the summer program, the classroom atmosphere was relaxed. Instead of the interrogation sessions that I had anticipated, the professors spoke informally, inviting our comments and questions. The reading assignments were reasonable, although I read the chapters twice for fear of missing something. I wanted to believe that I had a grip on things, but I didn't trust myself. During Monday's economics lectures my mind built questions on top of questions while everyone else took the information in stride. On Wednesdays, during the smaller class, I'd watch for signs of confusion as the professor's explanations darted from theory to formula to graph. My classmates wrote sparingly, nodded comprehendingly, and on top of it, spat back comments like they had spent their whole lives pondering the downhill slope of a supply curve.

I tried getting feedback from Niels to see how he was doing with his classes. Niels was no help unless "Let's check out this concert" counted as help. Good old Niels. I had to hand it to him. He opened his books, but not like I had to. Niels was at ease with the flow of things. Just like I used to skim through a semester's worth of school notes over the weekend and come up with an ace in high school, Niels could wing it at Princeton.

I missed the good old days. I missed the confidence. Unlike my roommate, I was at the foot of an uphill climb. I had already seen a D up close over the summer. I had even seen the big bad F. I'd seen my words squashed into nothingness with me rolled up in them. I had been given the look that I used to give to a complete dunce. The steady trickle of sweat while I studied confirmed that I was near, if not on, the bottom rung. The more I sweated, the more I was afraid, the harder I pressed.

I just didn't want to get caught without a clue when midterms came. I couldn't help thinking where I would be if I had been studying like this all along. Probably running the class instead of being a silent follower.

School had always been too easy. I had approached everything like simple math. Stare at a problem long enough and you can do it in your head. Dress it up and you were over! Up until very recently dealing with people had been simple math, too.

I wished I could go back and make things different, especially with the people I used to divide and subtract. I wished I could go back in time for a lot of things. I wouldn't be sweating like this if I had carried my load all along. I wouldn't feel like I was carrying it all alone.

Now I had to carry double. Do everything step by step. No

shortcuts. No fast formulas. The days of simple math were over.

We were reviewing the reading assignment in my economics class before moving on. For one moment, I thought I knew something and started to throw my hat in the ring. I pulled back at the last minute, though, and instead resorted to my usual dodge maneuver: dive straight into the lines of my notebook, as if searching for something. This was hard to do in economics, being so close to the line of scrimmage—especially when it finally occurred to the professor that he hadn't heard my voice since the semester began. Could I describe the relationship between inflation and unemployment?

I fit the explanation within a four-word answer.

The professor then went off on a tirade about politicians, and why we should keep the inevitable relationship between unemployment and inflation first and foremost in our minds during election time. Then he asked me to give an example of unrealistic economic policy with this in mind.

I shook my head, indicating that I couldn't. He was disappointed and called on one of the hands wanting recognition.

"I can't because I don't agree with you," I spoke up. "I think you *can* beat inflation without hurting the economy. Let me put it down in chalk." I knew I was wrong, but I could draw a reasonable possibility that I could argue in at least three rounds before all of my cards and equations were exhausted.

I knew it would be safer to spit back what he wanted, but I just couldn't do it. He had given me the simplest question as a kind of sympathetic pat on the head. A chance to open my mouth before the real class discussion got under way. But, even though I had to work harder than everyone else, I was no dummy. I wouldn't ever let anyone pat me on the head for giving the right answer when I knew there was a better one.

So there I went, swimming against the current, taking my long-term economic plan up to the board just to be contrary. It didn't matter that it would be shot down. What mattered was how long I would last and that I was capable of original thought based on what I had read. My instinct to debate wouldn't allow me to follow the rules or simply report what I had read. I mean, what good was any of it if your mind couldn't wrestle with it, and if you just read and accepted it because it was on the page? Did Vernon Watson raise me to play back someone else's words? Of course not.

I hogged all the blackboard with three graphs to outline various phases of my plan. A hand shot up in opposition. She spotted an error in my second graph. I came back at her, which silenced her for a minute. She withdrew, but only to regroup for another skirmish. That was cool.

The professor was enjoying the whole show. I had succeeded in turning the discussion into a debate. That only wound me up tighter, and from then on I couldn't stop. The icing was being able to support my thoughts with the material I had read. Not just talk off the top of my head, but lay down theorems: If this, then that, and therefore . . . *Yeah, I be workin!* Logic is like an arrow. You aim it and it shoots them all down, row after row.

As soon as class was over I ran to Firestone Library. I had to review the information listed in the appendix at the end of the chapter. I had to be prepared for the next class. I knew I was setting myself up, but challenge was about the only thing I respected. After all, I was my father's son.

I read through dinner. When hunger caught up to me I went for a walk. A group of students was headed in the same direction down William Street. I looked closer and saw Arnold. I ran after him.

"Arnold!"

Arnold was shocked to see me. Neither one of us had thought I'd be a freshman at Princeton this fall. I recognized other faces from the summer program. They seemed glad to see me, but not half as glad as I was to see them. I couldn't explain it, especially since I wasn't tight with anyone, not even with my ex-roommate Arnold, whom I came this close to embracing. Maybe it was that we had survived the summer program, and were still hanging in there. Maybe we spoke the same language.

"Where have you been?" I asked. "I haven't seen anyone in the past two weeks."

"We've all been split up—distributed to different dorms, different colleges," Arnold said.

"It's all part of the master plot," said Imhotep, whom I remembered from the summer program as being one of the "sheep" who had so easily denounced their intelligence. I never suspected he would be the one. Every class has one—the revolutionary Black thorn in White America's side. Back in the good old days it was Vernon.

"So where are you all going?" I asked.

"Over to the Third World Center," Arnold said. "You should come."

There was a brochure from the Center in my orientation folder, but I never looked at it. I didn't want to appear uninformed by asking what it was about, so instead I asked where it was.

"On the dark side of planet P," some students said together. Apparently, that was a question always asked, and a response always given. This turned out to be the serious truth. You had to be motivated to take that journey across campus.

I could tell from the conversation that they were all sufficiently motivated to get there, eager for the start of the activities. A play was being produced by the upperclassmen for the benefit of the freshmen. Already it stank of condescension. I went with them anyway.

We arrived at an oddly designed building on Olden Street and went inside. I expected to see symbols of "the struggle" all over the place or cultural relics that my dad would love. Instead, it was like walking into someone's living room. It was already packed with freshmen and upperclassmen waiting for the play to get started.

There was something about being there that I liked right away. It wasn't the overpowering place that I thought it would be. It was comfortable, like a small slice of home.

Before the play got under way members of the governance board spoke about the agenda for the year. We freshmen were advised repeatedly to take advantage of the tutorial services sponsored by the upperclassmen. Then campus life survival kits with information were given out to all freshmen and transfer students.

Finally, we were seated in the gallery for the play. It was about a guide leading a group of blind men through a jungle. Not very deep, but it was kind of entertaining. It reminded me of some of those plays my father would drag me to and mutter, "Right on, brother, right on," through all the acts. I used to slink down in my seat in total embarrassment. Then they stopped making those kinds of plays, or my father stopped taking me.

To my surprise, I found myself enjoying this play. It was the second act that got to me. During their journey, one of the blind men was distracted by the campus whirlwind and spent eternity wandering a circular path as an eternal freshman.

They didn't have to explain eternal freshman. I knew exactly what that was. I had seen one the other day on my way to class. A girl was standing at the bus stop on Nassau Street with her suitcases. She wasn't coming back.

She must have gotten snared by the campus whirlwind or was overwhelmed by the work. I'd have been standing right there beside her had I not gone through the summer program. It was too easy to get blinded. Everywhere you turned there were flyers announcing parties, lectures, games, and meetings. When there wasn't the constant motion of activities, there was the loneliness as you waited for the next activity.

Sometimes I'd feel loneliness creeping up on me. I wrote letters. I became pretty good at it. I wrote to anyone who could read and write back. I'd go to my mailbox two or three times a day, anxious for a piece of home. When the letters came I read them over and over. I never threw a letter out. I valued every word. Letters from Nana, Cousin Randy, Jonelle, and anyone else who remembered me kindly, or even not so kindly. Mostly I counted on my sister, Kerri, for five-page letters about her silly little world. My parents misinterpreted my pleas for mail as pleas for money, and would send a thin envelope. There was not a whole lot you could read into two lines and a check. They thought they were giving me my space. I wished they'd cut it out.

Wendy called, but not enough. Niels and I still went to dinner and a few games here and there, but he was caught up in his groove and I was trying to find mine. I wouldn't have minded hanging out with Arnold or any of the crew from the summer program, but being in different colleges made that almost impossible.

I got a tutor through the Third World Center. I didn't need one, but it was someplace to go on a regular basis. Then, too, I'd run into someone from the summer program over at the center or meet new folk.

My studies began to pick up, but I never relaxed. Not for one moment.

Once I felt in control of myself I could honestly say I liked being in school. All the same, I was looking forward to going home for Thanksgiving—even though I'd probably come home glad to see everyone and then within an hour be looking at the bus schedule and marking off the days on the calendar. It wouldn't take the folks long to work my nerves. They couldn't help it.

I got back my economics essay exam before the Thanksgiving break. I couldn't wait to show it to the folks. It would blow their minds. Not because of the grade, or the contents, but because of how I signed the honor statement. Every word on the exam that preceded the honor statement was the culmination of my sweat and brain, not a lot of hype. I liked that feeling of being able to take a theory, a graph, or an equation, blend it with my own thoughts, and then fly high with it. I was supposed to have knowledge and make things happen. Big things. It was there in my essays. There was no better way to sign the honor statement at the end of the exam than in my given name, Dinizulu.

I got on the bus to New York holding the blue booklet, rolled diploma tight. I wondered if the folks would dig the significance of my honor statement, or if they'd only see the letter A. Dad, I gave more credit. It would mean the world to him that I was signing my work in the name he had given me. Mom and Nana Dee would calmly dismiss it as a phase, but would call often next semester to check up on me. The only one who would miss it, for a change, was Kerri, who had always called me Dinizulu. One day, when her experience catches up with her brain, I'll open up to her, brother to sister, because I love her.

The main thing was I was home free. I had thrown down the mask and was ready to fly. Whether the world was ready or not was another story.

ABOUT THE AUTHOR

Author RITA WILLIAMS-GARCIA says, "I wrote *Fast Talk on a Slow Track* for the bright young men in my freshman class in college who were suddenly caught off guard by failure. The ones with half a chance confronted it head on. The others are still running."

The author grew up in Seaside, California, and Jamaica, New York. She is a graduate of Hofstra University and is pursuing her master's degree at Queens College. She lives in Jamaica, New York, with her husband and two daughters. Ms. Williams-Garcia is also the author of the Starfire novel, *Blue Tights* and is at work on her third novel.